In A Green Shade
A Country Commentary

by

Maurice Hewlett

Double9
BOOKS

In a green shade
A country commentary
by Maurice Hewlett

ISBN: 978-93-65785-97-5

Published by

DOUBLE 9 BOOKS
2/13-B, Ansari Road
Daryaganj, New Delhi – 110002
info@double9books.com
www.double9books.com
Tel. 011-40042856

ABOUT THE AUTHOR

In the late 19th and early 20th centuries, British author, poet, and essayist Maurice Henry Hewlett made significant contributions to historical fiction. Hewlett was educated at the University College School in London and studied at the British Museum. He was born on February 22, 1861, in Weymouth, England. His historical novels, which are frequently set in the mediaeval or Renaissance eras, brought Hewlett notoriety. "The Forest Lovers" (1898), a retelling of the Robin Hood story, and "The Life and Death of Richard Yea-and-Nay" (1900), a novel based on the life of Richard the Lionheart, are two of his most well-known works. His narratives were engrossing because he combined poetic language with an acute awareness of historical fact. Even though Hewlett's fame waned in the last decades of the 1900s, his creations were warmly embraced while he was alive. On June 15, 1923, Maurice Hewlett passed suddenly. He left behind a corpus of work that demonstrated his love of literature, history, and narrative.

CONTENTS

NOTE

All of these Essays, with two exceptions, have been published periodically. All, without exception, have been revised and corrected. My thanks for hospitality afforded to them *en route* are due to the *Westminster Gazette, Daily News,* and *Daily Chronicle;* to the *New Statesman;* to the *Cornhill Magazine, Fortnightly Review, Anglo-French Review,* and *London Mercury.*

BROADCHALKE, 22 Jan. 1920.

ROUND ABOUT A PREFACE

The title has become equivocal, since there are more green shades in employment now than were dreamed of by Andrew Marvell. Science is a great maker of homophones, without respect for the poets. There is, for instance, the demilune of lined buckram borne by the weak-eyed on their foreheads, the phylactery of the have-beens—I lay myself open to be believed a cripple, or to look an old fool. A vivacious reviewer in *Punch's* "Booking Office," will have a vision of me as a babbling elder peering at society from below a green pent. However—I must risk it. It says exactly what I mean; and what I have written I have written.

The point is that, having worked hard for a good many years, I can now consider my latter end under conditions favourable to leisurely and extended thought, sometimes in a garden made, if rightly made, in my own image, sometimes in a house which was built aforetime, in a day when men wrought for posterity as well as for themselves. In such seed-plots it is impossible that one's thoughts should not take colour as they rise. Whithersoever I look I see as much permanency as is good for any sojourner upon earth; I see embodied tradition, respect for Nature's laws, attention to beauty, subservience to use; all this within doors. Outside, the trees, the flowers are my calendar; the birds chime the hours; periodically the church-bell calls the travellers home. Between all these friendly monitors it is hard if one cannot keep the mean. If the passing-bell tempts me to moralise overmuch I may turn to the creatures, and learn to live for the moment. I should be slow to confess how much worldly wisdom I have won from what we choose to call the lower orders of creation, because nobody willingly betrays the whereabouts of his buried treasure, or the amount of it. Mr. Pepys, I remember, forgot both on a certain occasion, and had a devil of a time until he recovered his hoard. But my wealth was not made with hands, or not with my hands.

My house is fortunately placed, too, in the village street, so that I am in touch with my neighbours and their daily concerns, which I make mine so far as they are pleased to allow it. I am aware of them all day long by half a hundred signs; I know the trot of their horses, the horns of their motor-cars—that shows that there are not too many of them—the voices of their children, the death-shrieks of their pigs, the barking of their dogs. Not a day passes but one or other is in, to have some paper signed, to air a grievance, or to ask advice. The vicar and the minister are my good friends, and, I am glad to say, each other's. The farmers understand my ways (it is as much as I can expect of them), and the labourers like them. All this keeps the pores of the mind open; you cannot stagnate if you are useful to other people. Nor—unless you are a fool—can you be strict with your categories. The more you know of men and systems the more overlapping you see. I could not now, for my life, pigeonhole my acquaintance in this village of five hundred souls. "I have now been in Italy two days," Goethe wrote, "and I think I know my Italians pretty well!" When he had been there two years he knew better.

If ever there is a time for sententiousness it is when one is elderly, leisured and comfortable; that is the time to set down one's thoughts as they come, not inviting anybody to read them, but promising to those who do, that they will find a commentary upon life as it passes, either because it may be useful or because it may have been earned. I hope I have neither prejudice nor afterthought; I know that I have, as we say now, neither axe to grind nor log to roll. Politics! None. I want people to be happy; and whether Mr. George make them so, or the Trade Unions, whether Christ or Sir Conan Doyle, it's all one to me. I have my pet nostrums, of course. I believe in Poverty, Love, and England, and am convinced that only through the first will the other two thrive. I want men to be gentlemen and women to be modest. I want men to have work and women to have children. Any check on production, Trade-Union, war, or something else, will get no good words from me. As for war, after our late experience, I confess that I could be a Mr. Dick with it, but we are not apt in the country to dwell overmuch on war now it is over. We honour our beloved dead; those of us who have returned unbattered go now about our work with cooler, more critical eyes, but mostly with lips closed against our three or four years' experience. Khaki has disappeared; the war is over; let us forget it. If there is a people to be pitied, swarming and groping on this tormented earth, we say, it is the German people; but that seems an insufficient reason for hating them *in sæcula sæculorum*. A German is a human being, and very likely Mr. Bottomley is one too, and not a big-head in a pantomime; such also may be Mrs. Partington's nephew and the editor of the *Morning Post*. There does not seem much difference between them, and we must be charitable.

The sojourner in the green shade will find himself, as I have found myself, more interested in people (but not those people) than in books. We have too many books, as I discovered when I left London for good. I sold six tons, and again another six, when, after two years in West Sussex, I came home. Now I have collected about me the things I can't do without, the things of which I read at least portions every year, as well as a few which it is good to have handy in case of accidents. Book-collecting is a foppery, a pastime of youth, when spending money is as necessary as taking exercise, and you are better for an object in each case. But I find that I now read with motives other than those of old. I am now more interested in the author than in his book. That must mean that I am more interested in life than in art. I am reading at this moment Professor Child's edition of the Ballads, and though I am occasionally moved to tears by the beauty and tragic insight of things like *The Wife of Usher's Well*; *Clerk Saunders*, or *Lord Thomas and Fair Annie*, I am sure that considerations altogether unliterary move me more — such, for instance, as curiosity to know who composed, and for whom they composed, these lovely tales. I don't suppose that we shall ever know the name, or anything of the personality of any one poet of them. Those poets were as anonymous as our church-builders, and if they were content to be so we should be content to have it so. But one would be happy to know of what kind they were, and perhaps even happier (certainly I should) to realise their auditors. Did they write for men or women? That is one of my consuming quests. The staves of the *Iliad* were for men: that seems certain. Those of the *Odyssey* not so certainly. But take this from *May Collin*, and consider it.

You know the story, how "She fell in love with a false priest, and rued it ever mair"? The priest followed her "butt and ben," and gave her no peace. They took horses and money and rode out together "Until they came to a rank river, Was raging like the sea." There the priest declared his purpose:

"Light off, light off now, May Collin,
It's here that you must dee;
Here I have drown'd seven kings' daughters,
The eighth now you must be."

So her torture begins. He bids her cast off "her gown that's of the green," because it is too good to rot in the sea-stream; next her "coat that's of the black "; next her "stays that are well-laced"; lastly her "sark that's of the holland" — all for the same reason. Then the girl speaks:

"Turn you about now, false Mess John,
To the green leaf of the tree;
It does not fit a mansworn man
A naked woman to see."

The point is that he obeys her. She catches him round the body and flings him into the tide. *Women were listening to that tale.*

If I am to deal with life it must be in my own way, for there's no escape from one's character. I may be a good poet or a bad one—that's not for me to say; but I am a poet of sorts. Now a poet does not observe like a novelist. He does not indeed necessarily observe at all until he feels the need of observation. Then he observes, and intensely. He does not analyse, he does not amass his facts; he concentrates. He wrings out quintessences; and when he has distilled his drops of pure spirit he brews his potion. Something of the kind happens to me now, whether verse or prose be the Muse of my devotion. A stray thought, a chance vision, moves me; presently the flame is hissing hot. Everything then at any time observed and stored in the memory which has relation to the fact is fused and in a swimming flux. Anon, as the Children of Israel said to Moses, "There came forth this calf." One cannot get any nearer, I believe; and while I do not pretend that I have said all there is to say about anything here, I shall maintain that I have said all that need be said about the things which I touch upon. In an essay, as in a poem, the half is greater than the whole, if it is the right half. If it is the wrong half, why, then the shorter it is the better.

As most of these commentaries were written during the year which is mercifully over, it would not have been possible, even if it had been sought, to avoid current topics. Why should a writer shrink from being called a journalist? He need not cease to be writer. But if he wishes to be true to his original calling, to make his hope and election sure, he must always be careful to seek the universal in the particular; and that is where your idealist has such a pull, for he can see nothing else. And if he does that he need not be afraid that the conventions of Time and Space will be a hindrance to his book's path. He will be readable a century hence; he will be readable in the Antipodes; and that is as near infinity as any of us, short of Chaucer and Shakespeare, need trouble about. In the country one reads, not skims, the daily paper; and if one's comments are leisurely, perhaps they are all the better. At any rate one is not tempted to see the end of the world in a strike, or a second Bonaparte in Signor d'Annunzio. To me that poet seems rather a comic-opera brigand. I suspect him of a green velvet jacket with a two-inch tail. But if you regard him *sub specie eternitatis*, then I fear we must see in him all Italy in epitome. That was how Italy went to war—but you must live in the country to understand things like that, out of range of the tumult and the shouting.

No more of Signor d'Annunzio here or elsewhere in these pages; but of ourselves and our needs somewhat. Nobody could have lived through last year without considering anxiously whither we are tending and with what pretence. As the occasion moved me I have said my say about those matters, and here the reader will have as much of it as I am ready just now to give him. This is perhaps some sort of an apology for what may be found hereafter of a hortatory kind. I may be charged with wanting to do people "good." Well, if trying to make them happy is trying to do them good, then I confess the charge. There is no doubt whatever that they are not happy now. They hate too many people, they pant and toil after the wrong things; they serve false gods and forget the true ones. That is what we think about it in the country; and I am of the country's opinion.

We need, it seems to me, many things — religion, love, work, seriousness and so on; but what we need most of all, as I believe, is to wash our hands. For five years they have been groping and wrenching in the vitals of other people. They are foul and we are still drunk with the reek. In God's name, let us wash and then we can begin to build up the world again. We see the need of that out in the country, but so far as I can judge by what I read or have seen of London, there's no notion of it there.

But there's not much about London in this book.

CHANGE AND THE PEASANTRY

A book which I shall never willingly be without, one of my minor classics, is *Idlehurst*. Published in 1898, its author John Halsham, it has a touch upon country things, the penetrating, pitiful and *tant soit peu* condescending touch upon them of one who is both scholar and recluse, fastidious but discerning. He reads our earth, cloudscape, landscape, season, foison, man and beast of the field, with the same wistfulness which women who have known sorrow exhibit for children who have not. Reading him again, however, last night, after the long interval of fever and unrest which the war has enforced, I found his pessimism troublesome. Sussex, so far as I know it, is not so degenerate as he seems to have found it; and surely since the war began he must have changed his mind. It is hard to remember 1898, or 1913 for that matter, but I happen to know that Sussex emptied itself of its young manhood, and voluntarily, because I went to live there for a while in 1915 and found the village of my choice bare of youth. But that was West Sussex, and John Halsham lives nearer London, in the forest region, as I judge, which is a part of the country overflowed and become suburban. I don't doubt but complete cockneyfication will be the ultimate fate of that country of deep loam and handsome women before many years are over. Going down to my village from London, I could not feel that I was in the country until I had passed Pulborough; and further east the same would hold good to Lewes.

But when Mr Halsham in his bitterness cries out that "the town has overflowed the country," meaning the whole country, and that "we are cockney from sea to sea," he is being tragic at the cost of truth. Would he drag Wiltshire and all the pastoral West into his turmoil? You may go about any of the villages here, watch the daily doings of the inhabitants, and feel confident that, practically, there has been no substantial change since the Norman Conquest. The "feeling" of the scene is the same as it always was, the outlook of the people, their habit of mind, is the same. The one apparent difference is in religion, and that is not a difference of substance but of accident. We have forgotten the Madonna and the Saints, who were taken away from us by violence. We still go to church, but they are not there any more. They were expelled with a fork: one Cromwell but completed what another began. And now it is late in the day: they can never be brought back. "Vestigia nulla" is true of religion as of every other human affair. But it was not them we worshipped. Rather it was what they stood for—which endures.

All this leads me away from John Halsham and *Idlehurst*. A good antidote to his extreme depression is to be found in another beautiful book which, if not a classic, will become one. I mean *A Shepherd's Life*, wherein Mr. Hudson reveals the very heart of pastoral Wilts. I went right through it only the other day, journeying from Sarum to Trowbridge on county business—Wishford, Wylye, Codford, Heytesbury, and so on to Melksham and Westbury—names which to us are symphonies. No change from the sempiternal round of country labour in those quiet hollows, though it is true that you saw soldiers in buff unloading railway trucks, and that the valley was lined with their wooden hutments. Soldiers, indeed, we have known ever since the Norman Conquest; but the country is bigger than they are, and they fall into its ways even as their huts fade into the shadows cast by its everlasting hills. Mr. Hudson, by the way, does not seem to have encountered a witch. We had one in this village a few years ago, and she may be here still, though I haven't come across her. She laid a malison on my chauffeur's potatoes—I had one once—and (as he told me) blighted the year's crop. He was digging in his garden when she, a dark-browed old woman with a beard, leaned over the gate and asked him for some kindling wood. He, a Swiss, who may not have understood her, waved her away, saying that he was busy. "You will get no good out of those taters," said she, and slippered away. That was five years ago.

John Halsham is fond of describing himself as a Tory, and perhaps really is one of those almost extinct mammalia. I had thought Professor Saintsbury the only one left. He, I understand, thinks that the Reform Act of 1832 was a great mistake, and dislikes Horace Walpole's Letters because their writer was a Whig. Then there is Mrs. Partington's nephew, who muses perhaps without method, but certainly not without malice, in *Blackwood* once a month. He is more Jingo than Tory. He has to bite somebody. I was amused the other day to consider his girding at Sir Alfred Mond, chiefly on the score that he had a German grandfather. It did not seem to have occurred to the man that the same terrific charge could be brought against a much more august Personage, and with much the same futility. Surely it is more to the purpose that he will have an English grandson, That is the worst of musing when you neglect method and surrender to malice.

Toryism, which is a parasitic growth of mind, needs a relic to which it can cling, not a person. In the country the Church will not provide it, nor any longer the brewing interest. The air has been let into the one, and the water which they call mineral into the other. There remain the throne and the squirearchy, and of these the throne is much the stouter. For the throne is remote enough to be an object of veneration, separable from its occupant; but when the great house and the old acres are held, and not filled, by a new man, the villager, who sees more than he is supposed to see, is by no means concerned to uphold them. Most of the villages have been Radical; now they are all going "Labour." The elections, if there are to be some soon, will be very interesting, and I think surprising to Mr. George and his assortment of friends.

However—another strike or two like that recent abortion on the railways will dish the Labour Party and Trade Unionism as well—at least in the country. Down here we are new to the movement, but have gone into it keenly, without losing our heads. Indeed, I think we are finding more in our heads than we suspected. We keep to our code; and when we find that other men don't, we begin to doubt of Unionism. One of the very best of our men said in my hearing at the time that if the railway strike were the kind of thing we were to expect, he, for one, would have no more to do with the Labourers' Union. As I have said once before, I think, responsibility (which the Union is giving us) deepens our men and quickens them too. The time is at hand when they will begin to feel their power. I have no fears. I have long known them to be the salt of the earth. If the quotation would not be from one of my own works, I would quote now.

It is an old discussion, but all my travels have convinced me that a bad peasantry is the exception. Such exceptions there are, though I don't mean to give them. If Zola had not made himself ridiculous in the act, so ridiculous as to show himself negligible, he would stand as the greatest traducer of his adopted country that France has ever harboured. But he was a specialist in his particular line of disgustfulness, and saw in rural France what he took there with him. They say that the Bulgarian peasant is a savage brute, "they" being the Greeks, of course. I would not mind betting a crown that he is nothing of the sort.

In manners, to be sure, peasantries differ remarkably. Here in the West, from Wilts to Cornwall, our rustics are sweet-mannered. They are instinctively gentlemen, if gentlehood consist, as I believe, in having regard for other people's feelings. But in the Danish parts of England, to be plain, manners are to seek. That means from Bedfordshire pretty well up to Carlisle. North-east of that again, in Northumberland, you have delightful manners.

The Northumbrian peasant, like the Scottish, greets you as an equal, the Wiltshire man as a superior, yet neither loses dignity thereby. The Lancashire man treats you as his inferior, and is not himself advantaged, whether it be so or not.

A HERMITAGE IN SIGHT

I hope that I have secured for myself a haven, a yet more impenetrable shade than this, against the time when, having seen four generations of men, two behind and two beyond, I may consider in silence what is likely to be the end of it all. It is true that I am getting old, but I am not yet prepared for a lodge in the wilderness. My present house has a wall on the village street. The post-office is a matter of crossing the road; the church is at the bottom of a meadow. I like all that, because I like all my neighbours and the sound of their voices. At eleven o'clock in the morning I can hear the children let out from school, "as shrill as swifts in upper air." That, too, I like. But the time will come when silence is best, and, as I say, I believe that I have found the very place. I have had my eye upon it for years, and seldom a month passes but I am there. A small black dog and I once saw Oreads there, or said we did, and in print at that. This very year the farm to which it belongs came into the market, and was sold; the purchaser will treat with me. I have described it once, nay twice, and won't do it again. Enough to say that it is the butt end of a deep green combe in the Downs, that it is sheltered from every wind, faces the south, and is below an ancient road, now a grass track, and the remains of what is called a British village on the ordnance maps, a great ramparted square with half a dozen gateways and two mist-pools within its ambit. All about it lie the neolithic dead, of whose race, as Glaucus told Diomede, "I boast myself to be."

We are all Iberians here, or so I love to believe, grounding myself upon the learned Dr. Beddoes—a swarthy people, dark-haired, grey-eyed, rather under than over the mean height. The aboriginal strain has proved itself stronger than the Frisian, and the Danish type does not appear at all. There are English names among us, of course, such as Gurd, which is Gurth as pronounced by a Norman; but it is understood that we are neolithic chiefly on the distaff side. The theory that each successive wave of invasion demolished the existing inhabitants is absurd. Not even the Germans do that; nor have the Turks succeeded in obliterating the Armenian nation. No—in turn our oncoming hordes, Celts, Romans, English, Danes, enslaved the men and married, or at least mated with, the women. And so we are descended, and (let me at this hour of victory be allowed to say) a marvellous people we are. For tenacity, patience, and obedience to the law—not of men, but of nature—I don't suppose there is another such people in the world.

Those characteristics, for which neither Celt nor Roman, Teuton nor Dane, as we know them now, is remarkable, I set to the score of the neolithic race, whose physical features are equally enduring.

When you get what seems like a clear case in either sex, you have a very handsome person.

The most beautiful woman I ever saw in my days was scrubbing a kitchen floor on her knees, when I saw her first—not a hundred miles from here. Pure Iberian, so far as one can judge—olive skin, black hair, grey-green eyes. Otherwise—colouring apart—the Venus of Milo, no less. I don't say that she was very intelligent. I wonder if the Venus was. But she was obedient to the law of her being—that I do know; and it is a matter of faith with me that Aphrodite can have been no less so.

Neither a quick-witted nor an imaginative race are we; but we have the roots of poetry in us, and the roots of other arts, for we have reverence for what is above and beyond us. Custom, too, we worship, and decency and order. We fight unwillingly, and are very slow to anger; but we never let go. Witness the last four dreadful years; witness Europe from Mons to Gallipoli. The British private, soldier or sailor, has been the backbone of the fight for freedom. But I am a long way from my valley in the Downs.

I shall first of all sink a well, for one must have water, even if one is going to die. Then I shall make a mist-pool—that art is not lost yet—because as well as water to drink I like water to look upon. Lastly, I will build a hermitage of puddled chalk and straw, and thatch it with reeds, if I can get them. It will consist of a single room thirty feet long. It will have a gallery at each end, attained by a ladder. In each gallery shall be a bed, and the appurtenance thereof, one for use and one for a co-hermit or hermitess, if such there be. I leave that open. There must be a stoop, of course. Nothing enclosed. No flowers, by request. The sheep shall nibble to the very threshold. I don't forget that there is a fox-earth in the spinney attached. I saw a vixen and her cubs there one morning as clearly as I see this paper. She barked at me once or twice, sitting high on her haunches, but the children played on without a glance at me. They were playing at catch-as-catch-can—with a full-grown hare. Sheer fun. No after-thoughts. I watched them for twenty minutes.

If I grow anything there at all I shall confine my part of the business to planting, and let Nature do the rest. It may be absolutely necessary to keep the sheep off for a year or two, and the rabbits—but that is all. And what I do plant shall be deciduous, so that I may have the yearly miracle to expect. It is a mighty eater of time—and there won't be much of that left probably; yet a joy which no man who has ever begotten anything, baby or poem, can deny himself.

If anybody wants to see what Nature can do in the way of a season's growth, I can tell him how to go to work. Let him plant on the bank of a running water a root of *Gunnera manicata*. Let him then wait ten years, observing these directions faithfully. Every fall, after the first frost—that frost which blackens his dahlias—let him cover the crown of his *Gunnera* with one of its own leaves. Pile some stable-stuff over that, and then heap upon all the leaf-sweepings of that part of the garden. Growth starts in mid-April and proceeds by feet a week. Mine, which is about ten years old now, is thirty-five feet in circumference, nearly twelve feet high, has flowers two-feet-six in length, and in a hot summer has grown leaves seven feet across. You can go under one of them in a shower of rain and be as dry as in church. And all that done in five months. The plant is a rhubarb of sorts and comes from Chili. I should like to see it over there on the marge of some monstrous great river. In another order, the *Ipomoea* (Morning Glory), which comes from East Africa, runs it close. I had one seed in Sussex which completely overflowed a garden wall, smothering everything upon it. A kind of Jack's beanstalk, and every morning starred with turquoise blue trumpet mouths of ravishing beauty, which were dead at noon. The poor thing was constrained to be a hierodule, gave no seed. Nature is the prodigal's foster-mother.

I have a plant whose seed is much more beautiful than its flower. By the way, I have two, for the Spindle Tree is in seed, which has a quite insignificant blossom. But the plant I mean is a wild peony, which I dug up in a brake on the slopes of Helikon. It is a single white whose flower lasts, perhaps, three days. It makes a large seed-pod, which burst a short time ago, and revealed blue-black seeds sheathed in coralline forms of the most absolute vermilion. You could see them fifty yards away. It seems to have no purpose in life but to pack the seeds—or perhaps, they are beacons for the birds. I took pains to be beforehand with the birds, having no desire to see Greek peonies in my neighbours' gardens. The seeds are safely bestowed, though their fate has not been Jonah's. There's a spinney of elder-trees in the combe of my hermitage, which, I am told, was planted entirely by magpies. And I suppose it was wood-pigeons who planted two ilex trees on the top of the Guinigi tower in Lucca; and some bird or other, once more, which is answerable for a fine fig-tree growing in the parapet of the bridge at Cordova, in no soil whatsoever. It was loaded with fruit when I saw it. But fig-trees are like poets; if you want them to sing you must torture their roots. The parallel wobbles, but will be understood.

DORIAN MODES

Being known in these parts for a friendly soul, and trusted, moreover, I have fallen into the position among the peasantry which the parson used to hold, and does still when he takes the trouble to qualify for it. If I can't always tell them what to do I may be able to put them in the way of the man who can. One learns how to make a dictionary of life as one gets on in it. Another use which they can have of me: I can tell them how to put their requests or demands. They have no sense whatever of a written language.

I must not betray confidences, or I could relate some curious matters on this head. I know, for instance, a farmer who is worth a couple of hundred thousand at the least, and who can neither write nor read. He has learned somehow a cross between a scratch and a blot which is accepted as a signature to cheques—but no more than that. And there is no harm in saying that I often need an interpreter. I had a case the other night when a man I know brought in a friend for consultation—a youth of the round-headed, flaxen, Teutonic type, rather rare here, who came from a village still more remote from the world than this one. Not one word of his fluent and frequent speeches could I understand. It was largely a question of intonation I believe—but there it was.

He had the wild, inspired look of a savage. He again could neither read nor write, though he must have been at school within the last ten or twelve years; but, as I think I have said elsewhere, it is not uncommon for boys to go through the school course and fail to pass the standards. There are here two families in particular, admirable workmen, who for two generations have left school without having acquired either writing or reading. One wonders deeply what kind of processes go on in the minds of these fine young men, steady workmen, as they are, good husbands, kind fathers, useful citizens oftener than not. What is their conception of God, of human destiny? How does Religion get at them? Or does it? Shall we ever know? Not if Mr. Hardy cannot tell us. No other poet of peasant origin has done so—neither Clare, nor Blomfield, nor even Burns. Mr. Hardy has told us something, and might have told us a good deal more if by the time he had learned his craft, he had not learned to be chiefly interested in himself. That is the way of poets.

Then there's *The Shropshire Lad*, a fake perhaps, since its author was not a peasant, but a divine little book. *The Shropshire Lad* is morbid, unless lads are so in Shropshire—in which case they, too, are morbid; but it is a golden book of whose beauty and felicity I never tire. Technically it is by far the most considerable thing since *In Memoriam*: "Loveliest of trees, the Cherry," makes me cry for sheer pleasure. But it is haunted by the fear of death and old age; it is afraid of love; it is sometimes cynical—none of which things are true of youth in Salop or Salonika. The young peasant is a fatalist to the core; but fatalists are not afraid of death. Youth is ephemeral and so is the young peasant. He is always happy when the sun is out.

As for love, it is truly the hot-and-cold disease with him. He is himself his "own fever and pain," like the rest of us; but I think love is a physical passion, until marriage. After marriage it may grow into something very beautiful indeed, and the more beautiful for being incapable of bodily utterance. I have a pair often under my eye down here who are, I know, all in all to each other; yet their conversation is that of two old gossips. But at fortunate moments I may induce one of them to tell of the other, and then you find out. My *Village Wife* was no imagination of mine. She lives and suffers not so many miles from where I write. Indeed, you may say of our peasantry very much what French people will tell you of their marriage custom, that love at its best follows that ceremony. It is not bred by romance, but by intimacy. The romantic attachment flames up, and satiety quenches it. The other kind glows red-hot but rarely breaks into a flame. You may have which you choose: you are lucky indeed if you get both.

To return, however, to dialect, intonation, as I say, has much to do with it. It is attractive, and in poetry can be very touching. I have had the advantage of hearing Barnes's poems read by a lady who has the accent perfectly. One does not know Barnes or Wessex who does not hear him read. That is true of all poetry, no doubt—but Barnes is uncommonly dull to read. As for words, we have enough of our own to support a small lexicon, which I used to possess, but have just been hunting, in vain. Perhaps after the pattern of the arrow, I shall find it again in the shelf of a friend. I remember that we call the roots of a tree the *mores*; that a dipper is a *spudgell*; that we say "*dout* the candle" when we mean extinguish it. We say "to-year" as you say "to-morrow," and call the month of March "Lide." February used to be "Soul-grove," but I have never heard it called so. The pole of a scythe is the *snead*; the two handles are the *nibs*. They are fastened by rings called *quinnets*. Isaac Taylor says that the few remaining Celtic words we have in use (other than hill or river names) are words for obscure parts of tools. We have some queer intensives—"terriblish" or "tarblish" is one, and "ghastly," meaning ugly, is another. "A terrible ghastly sight" we say, meaning that a thing looks rather ugly.

Our demonstrative pronoun is *thic,* or more properly *dhic;* "dhic meäd" means "that meadow." *Suent* means pleasant or proper—really both. It always has a sense of right consequence, of one thing following another as it ought. "Suently" would be "duly." But that now is common to the West, and will be heard from Land's End to Hengistbury Head, as well as in every one of Mr. Phillpotts' novels.

Doubtless it is too late to protest—since I am upon words—against a current barbarism which is at least ten years old, and against which I have publicly cried out at least twenty times. For the twenty-first time, then, let me object to "wage" for "wages." *Is* the wages of sin death, or *are* they? Do you give a man an alms, or an alm?

Shall we read—

Fear no more the heat o' the sun,
Nor the furious winter's *rage,*

and so on? Go to. But I shall not so easily convert Trade Union orators, Members of Parliament, Mr. Sidney Webb, or the *Times.* To them a wages is a wage, and an alms an alm, a man's riches his rich, and his breeches his—at least I suppose so. I wish that we could call a man's speeches his speech, and find it was perfectly true. It is a terrible thought, "a terrible ghastly thought" indeed, that we have not so long ago chosen over seven hundred persons of both sexes, each of whom will conceive it his right to make a speech in Parliament every day. Think of it. It is fair to suppose that every one of them will make one speech every year, many of them, no doubt, one every week, some certainly every day. I am thankful that I wasn't a candidate, for I might have been successful. Then I should have been compelled to listen, and perhaps tempted to reply, to some or all of those speeches. "In the end thereof despondency and madness."

CHURCH AND THE MAN

At our Peace Celebration the other day that happened which in my recollection never happened before. The entire village was in the parish church, sang *Te Deum*, prayed prelatical prayers, and shared *Hymns Ancient and Modern*. The Congregational Minister, in a black gown, read the Lesson, the Vicar, in surplice and stole, preached. All that in a village where more than half the people are Nonconformists, and done upon the mere motion of that particular section of us.

No experience since the War has touched me more; and I believe it is strongly symptomatic. Akin to it was the streaming of the people in London to Buckingham Palace, just when war was declared, and again on the day of the Armistice: both matters of pure instinct. For what do these things show except that we are children who, when we are moved, run to our mother to tell her all about it? What are we, when we are stripped to the soul, but one great family? A man told me once that he was present at a trial for murder where there were half a dozen in the dock, men and women, principals and accessories. The verdict was "Guilty," and the wretches stood up to receive the death-sentence. As they did so, by one common instinct, they all joined hands, and so remained until they were led away to the cells. A strangely moving scene.

It is by no means a necessity of the simple alone to seek a common expression of their hope and calling. A similar stream is carrying the learned which at present runs parallel with our homelier brook, but will sooner or later mingle waters. Then there will be a flood wherein many tired swimmers will doubtless perish, but which may lead to the sea those who keep their heads. Signs of that are on all sides of us. "*What is the Kingdom of Heaven?*" asks Mr. Clutton-Brock, and succeeds at his best in telling us what it is not. As for anything more positive, he concludes very reasonably that it is a state of mind, and leaves us to infer that the ruck of humanity need the guidance of inspiration to induce it.

It is not at all difficult for him to show that the Church lacks inspiration, or that there is something inherent in the essence of a Church destructive of it. What should have been equally easy would have been to point out that the Church's Founder as certainly had it. Nobody ever guided men more unfalteringly than He, and we need not doubt but that it was His instigation which turned the hearts of the village people to find a common focus for their thanksgiving. Mr. Clutton-Brock has felt the sting and owned to the need; he is in the stream, but is not a bold swimmer. I hope he may reach the sea.

Why it is—assuming the inspiration of Christ—that men have nevertheless ceased to be guided by it, and have consequently lost touch with the Kingdom of Heaven, is explained by a more hardy plunger in the stream, the Hibbert Lecturer upon *"Christ, Saint Francis, and To-day."* With great learning, skill and courage he has used the documents of the Franciscan revival to illustrate what must have happened to the Christian well-spring. He shows that even in the lifetime of its founder the Franciscan fraternity crystallised under the insensible but enormous pressure of the world, the flesh and (doubtless) the devil. Saint Francis of Assisi, for instance, taught literal poverty—abstinence from money, goods and books. His Franciscans wouldn't have it. They asked for money and took it. Not always directly, but always somehow.

"By God we owen forty pound for rent!" said Chaucer's Franciscan when pressed by the good wife to declare what ailed him; and he got his forty pound. Saint Francis told them to build churches like barns; they built them like cathedrals. He would have had men uninstructed in all but love; and they became the greatest schoolmen in Europe. The world, in fact, was too much with them. So also did Christ teach; and as the Franciscans modified their master's precepts, so did Saint Paul his.

Twice, then, the world has been demonstrably wrong. Is it a possibility that Christ and St. Francis can be proved to have been right? To those who say, as Mr. Clutton-Brock does, that Christianity has failed, I should like to retort, "Let Christianity be tried." Poverty is of the essence of it, and luckily for us poverty is coming upon us, nation and individuals, whether we deserve it or not. When we are all really poor together—in heart as well as purse—we shall have the chance of a common religion, but not till then. Now, then, comes the question: Can the high in heart become poor in heart, or the high-minded humble themselves? If it is hard for the man rich in goods to enter the Kingdom of Heaven, is it not still harder for the man stored with knowledge? How are Mr. Clutton-Brock and the Hibbert Lecturer to become as little children? How will Mr. Wells manage it? He, too, is in the stream, splashing about and apparently enjoying himself. But you may call an invisible God an invisible king, if you please, and yet be no nearer the heart of the matter. A change of definitions will not do it. And what of Sir Oliver Lodge and Sir Conan Doyle? Are their outpourings symptomatic? I don't myself think so. They are concerned with a future life, whereas those who seek a common religion will take no account of life at all, past, present or to come, once they have found the Kingdom of Heaven. Those eloquent and (I trust) sincere gospellers are agog to dispel that sense of loss which besets us just now. It is not that we fear death so much, but that we miss the dead—and no wonder. Hence these prophets crying Lo here! and Lo there! That they have reassured many I know well, that they have baffled others I know also, for they have baffled me. My puzzle is that, with evidence of authenticity difficult to withstand, the things they can find to report are so trivial. The test of a revelation I take to be exactly the same as the test of a good poem. It doesn't much matter whether the thing revealed is new or not. Is it so revealed that we needs must believe it? Relevance is to the point, compatibility is to the point. But when Sir Oliver Lodge's medium puts whisky and cigars into the mouth of the dead, we don't laugh: it is too serious for that. We change the conversation.

Steadfastness in mutability, that is the common need, a Rock of Ages.

> Then 'gin I thinke on that which Nature sayd,
> Of that same time when no more change shall be,
> But stedfast rest of all things, firmely stayd
> Upon the pillars of Eternity,
> That is contrayr to Mutabilitie;
> For all that moveth doth in change delight:
> But thenceforth all shall rest eternally
> With Him that is the God of Sabaoth hight:
> O! that great Sabaoth God, grant me that Sabaoth's sight.

BESSY MOORE

"My best wishes and respects to Mrs. Moore; she is beautiful. I may say so even to you, for I was never more struck with a countenance." That is Byron, writing to Tom Moore in 1812, when he had been married little more than a year—and Byron's opinion of woman's beauty is worth having. In the eight volumes of Tom's memoirs, worthily collected by his friend Lord John Russell, and in all the crowded stage of it, I see no figure shining in so sweet and clear a morning light as that of his little home-keeping wife, with her "wild, poetic face," her fancy which rings always truer than Tom's own, and her mother-love, which sorrow has to sound so deeply before she can leave the scene. Her appearances are fitful; she keeps to the hearth when the grandees hold the floor. You see nothing of her at Holland House, which Tom may use as his inn, or at Bowood, if she can help herself, which in the country is his house of call. She is the Jenny Wren of this little cock-robin; she wears drab, too often mourning; but you find that she counts for very much with Tom. He loves to know her at his back, loves to remind himself of it. He is always happy to be home again in her faithful arms. Through all the sparkle and flash, under all the talk, through all the tinklings of pianos and guitars which declare Tom's whereabouts, if you listen you can hear the quiet burden of her heart-beats. I don't know what he would have done without her, nor what we should have to say to his literary remains if she were not in them to make them smell of lavender. Few men of letters, and no wits, can have left more behind, with less in them.

There is a great deal less of Bessy in the memoirs than, say, of Lady Donegal, or of Rogers, or of Lord Lansdowne, but somehow or another she makes herself felt; and though her appearances in them are of Tom's contrivance, a personality is more surely expressed than in most of his more elaborate portraits. One gets to know her as indeed the "excellent and beautiful person" of Lord John's measured approval, not so much by what she says or does as by her reactions on Tom himself. A study of her has to be made out of a number of pencil-scratches—one here, one there—put down by the diarist with unpremeditated art; for it is certain that, though Moore intended his diaries to speak for him after his death, what he had to say of his wife was the last thing in them he would have relied upon to do it. I am sure that is so; nevertheless, with the exception of Tom himself, who, of course, holds the centre of the stage, she is more surely and sensibly there than any of his thousand characters, from the Prince Regent to the poet Bowles; more surely and fragrantly there. We are the better for her presence; and so is her Tom's memory, infinitely the better.

It was a secret marriage and, except in the minds of a few good judges, an improvident.

> "I breakfast with Lady Donegal on Monday," he writes to his mother in May, 1811, "and dine to meet her at Rogers' on Tuesday; and there is to be a person at both parties whom you little dream of."

This person was Bessy, to whom he had been married some two months on the day of writing, and of whom, when his family was notified, he found that it had nothing good to say. He complains of disappointment, of a "degree of coldness" in his father's comments; and neither is perhaps very wonderful. For Miss Bessy not only had nothing a year, but in the reckoning of the day, and in comparison with the young friend of Lord Moira and Lady Donegal, she herself was nothing. She was indeed a professional actress—Miss E. Dyke in the play-bills—whom Tom had first met in 1808 when the Kilkenny Theatre began a meteor-course. He had lent himself as an amateur to the enterprise, was David in *The Rivals*, Spado (with song) in *A Castle of Andalusia*. In 1809, for three weeks on end, he had been Peeping Tom of Coventry to the Lady Godiva of Miss E. Dyke. The rest is easy guessing, and so it is that Tom's parents were dismayed, and that there was a "degree of coldness." Lady Godiva, indeed!

But Bessy was not long in showing herself as good as gold, or approving herself to some of Tom's best friends. Lady Donegal and her sharp-tongued sister, Mary Godfrey, both took to her. "Give our love, honest, downright love to Bessy," they write. Rogers called her Psyche, had the pair to stay with him, stayed with them in his turn, and gave Bessy handsome sums for the charities in which she abounded all her life. Rogers knew simplicity when he saw it, and had no vitriol on hand when she was in the way. I don't think Tom ever took her to Ireland with him, or that, consequently, she ever met his parents in the flesh; but no doubt that they accepted her, and esteemed her.

Bit by bit she reveals herself in Tom's random diaries. As in the printing of a photograph the lights and darks come sparsely out, and unawares the delicate outline, so by a word here, a phrase elsewhere, we realise the presence of a sweet-natured, sound-minded girl, and more than that, of a girl with character. After a spell of Brompton lodgings Tom took her to Kegworth in Leicestershire, where he was to have the neighbourhood and countenance of his patron of the moment, Moira, the Regent's jackal, a solemn, empty-headed lord. Donington Hall and Bessy appear together in a letter to Mary Godfrey.

> "… I took Bessy yesterday to Lord Moira's, and she was not half so much struck with its grandeur as I expected. She said, in coming out, 'I like Mr. Rogers's house ten times better.'"

Tom feels it necessary to explain such remarkable taste. "She loves everything by association, and she was very happy in Rogers's house." I don't know whether Tom's simplicity or Bessy's is the more remarkable in all this. Tom's, I think.

"Lady Loudoun and Lord Moira called upon us on their way to town and brought pine apples, etc." One sees them at it; and the very next letter he writes is dated "Donington Park." Tom fairly lets himself go over it.

> "… I think it would have pleased you to see *my wife* in one of Lord Moira's carriages, with his servant riding after her, and Lady Loudoun's crimson travelling-cloak round her to keep her comfortable. It is a glorious triumph of good conduct on both sides, and makes my heart happier and prouder than all the best worldly connections could possibly have done. The dear girl and I sometimes look at each other with astonishment in our splendid room here, and she says she is quite sure it must be all a dream."

Marble halls, in fact; but let us see how it acted upon Bessy. Shortly after: "… I am just returned from a most delightful little tour with Rogers, poor Bessy being too ill and too fatigued with the ceremonies of the week to accompany us." That was to be the way of it for the rest of their lives together. She would never go to the great houses if she could by any means avoid it, but bore him no grudge for going without her, and was always open-armed for his return.

> Mayfield Cottage, Ashbourne, was their next harbourage; and here is a Wheatley picture of them on their way to a dinner-party.

> "We dined out to-day at the Ackroyds', neighbours of ours … we found, in the middle of our walk, that we were near half an hour too early, so we set to practising country-dances in the middle of a retired green lane till the time was expired."

Then he takes her to the Ashbourne ball, and for once leaves himself out of the letter.

"… You cannot imagine what a sensation Bessy excited at the Ball the other night. She was prettily dressed, and certainly looked very beautiful…. She was very much frightened, but she got through it very well. She wore a turban that night to please me, and she looks better in it than anything else; for it strikes everybody almost that sees her, how like the form and expression of her face are to Catalani's, and a turban is the thing for that kind of character."

Catalani, in Caverford's portrait, has the rapt eye of the Cumæan sibyl. One of Moore's fine friends, an admirer of Bessy's, speaks to him of her "wild, poetic face," and the Duchess of Sussex thought her like "Lady Heathcote in the days of her beauty." That is putting her very high, for, according to Cosway, Lady Heathcote was a lovely young woman indeed; but the "wild, poetic face" gets us as near as need be.

In 1815 troubles began from which the poor girl was never to be free again. She lost one of her three little girls, Olivia Byron, for whom the poet had been sponsor. "… It was with difficulty I could get her away from her little dead baby," Moore tells his mother, "and then only under a promise that she should see it again last night…." In 1817, while Moore was in Paris, pursuing his pleasures, another child, Barbara, had a fall, and he came home in August to find her "very ill indeed." On September 10th she is still ill, but if she should get a little better, "I mean to go for a day or two to Lord Lansdowne's to look at a house…. He has been searching his neighbourhood for a habitation for me, in a way very flattering indeed from such a man." But he did not go. September 20th, "It's all over, my dearest Mother!"

"Poor Bessy," we read, "neither eats nor sleeps enough hardly to sustain life": nevertheless in the first week of October he is at Bowood. "I arrived here the day before yesterday, and found Rogers, Lord and Lady Kerry, etc." He saw Sloperton Cottage and stayed out his week. Bessy then had to see the cottage, and went—but not from Bowood. "Bessy, who went off the night before last to look at the cottage near Lord Lansdowne's, is returned this morning, after travelling both nights. Power went with her." In a month's time they were in possession, and Tom vastly set up by the near neighbourhood of his exalted friend. Not so, however, his Jenny Wren.

"… We are getting on here as quietly and comfortably as possible, and the only thing I regret is the want of some near and plain neighbours for Bessy to make an intimacy with, and enjoy a little tea-drinking now and then, as she used to do in Derbyshire. She contrives, however, to employ herself very well without them; and her favourite task of cutting out things for the poor people is here even in greater requisition than we bargained for, as there never was such wretchedness in any place where we have been; and the better class of people (with but one or two exceptions) seem to consider their contributions to the poor-rates as abundantly sufficient, without making any further exertion towards the relief of the poor wretches. It is a pity Bessy has not more means, for she takes the true method of charity—that of going herself into the cottages, and seeing what they are most in want of.

"Lady Lansdowne has been very kind indeed, and has a good deal won me over (as you know, kindness *will* do now and then). After many exertions to get Bessy to go and dine there, I have at last succeeded this week, in consequence of our being on a visit to Bowles's, and her having the shelter of the poet's old lady to protect her through the enterprise. She did not, however, at all like it, and I shall not often put her to the torture of it. In addition to her democratic pride— which I cannot blame her for—which makes her prefer the company of her equals to that of her superiors, she finds herself a perfect stranger in the midst of people who are all intimate; and this is a sort of dignified desolation which poor Bessy is not at all ambitious of. Vanity gets over all these difficulties; but pride is not so practicable."

Vanity indeed did, though Tom had a pride of his own too. But he was soothed and not offended by pomp, whereas she was bored as well as irritated. It is obvious that her wits were valid enough. She could be happy with Rogers or the Bowleses, who could allow for simplicity, and delight in it—a talent denied to the good Lansdownes. As for Bowles, Tom is shrewd enough to remark upon "the mixture of talent and simplicity in him."

"His parsonage-house at Brenthill is beautifully situated; but he has a good deal frittered away its beauty in grottos, hermitages and Shenstonian inscriptions. When company is coming he cries, 'Here, John, run with the crucifix and missal to the hermitage, and set the fountain going.' His sheep-bells are tuned in thirds and fifths."

Such was Bowles, Bessy's best friend in Wilts.

Bowood to Tom was centre of his scheme of things; he was always there on some pretext or other; or he would dine and sleep at Bowles's or at Lacock Abbey, or spend days in Bath, or a week in London. It is true that half his talent and more than half his fame were social: these things were the bread as well as the butter of life to him. But here is Bessy meantime:

> "… Came home and found my dearest Bessy very tired after her walk from church. She has been receiving the Sacrament, and never did a purer heart.… In the note she wrote me to Bowles's the day before, she said, 'I am sorry I am not to see you before I go to church.'"

Tom had sensibility, not a doubt of it; but it seems to me that she had something better.

Here again, on the 16th October, "My dear Bessy planting some roots Miss Hughes has brought her, looking for a place to put a root of pink hepatica in, where (as she said) 'I might best see them in my walk.'" Yes, he had sensibility; but she had imagination. A little Tom was born a week after that. She took it badly, as she did most of her labours, and was in bed a month. On the 18th November she went out for the first time after the event—"the day delightful." She "went round to all her flower-beds to examine their state, for she has every little leaf in the garden by heart." Tom himself had been much moved by the birth of his first boy. He was called up at 11.30, sent for the midwife, was upset, walked about half the night, thanked God—"the maid, by the way, very near catching me on my knees." She might have caught Bessy on them every day, and no thought taken of so simple a thing. But Tom had sensibility.

But a man who, eight years after marriage, can make his wife an April fool, and record it, is no bad husband, and it would be a trespass on his good fame to suggest it. He loved her dearly and could never have been unkind to her. Far from that, happy domestic pictures abound in his diaries. Here is one of a time when she had joined him in London, on her way to stay with her sister in Edinburgh. They went together to Hornsey, to see Barbara's grave. "At eight o'clock she and I sauntered up and down the Burlington Arcade, then went and bought some prawns and supped most snugly together." He takes the state-rooms costing £7 apiece, for "his own pretty girl." Meantime he is preparing to shelter in France from civil process served upon him for the defalcations of his deputy in Bermuda.

I need not follow the scenes through as they come. The essence of Bessy Moore is expressed in what I have written of the first flush of her married life. There was much more to come. Moore outlived all his children, and she, poor soul, outlived her rattling, melodious Tom, having known more sorrow than falls, luckily, to the lot of most mothers. The death of her last girl, Anastasia, is beautifully told by Tom; but a worse stroke than even that was the wild career of little Tom, the son, his illness, disgrace, and death in the French Foreign Legion. That indeed went near to breaking Bessy's heart. "Why do people sigh for children? They know not what sorrow will come with them." That is her own, and only recorded, outcry.

> In *The Loves of the Angels*, an erotic and perfervid poem, which fails, nevertheless, from want of concentration of the thought, Zeraph, the third angel, is Tom himself, and the daughter of man, Nama, with whom he consorts, is Bessy.

> Humility, that low, sweet root,
> From which all heavenly virtues shoot,
> Was in the hearts of both—but most
> In Nama's heart, by whom alone
> Those charms for which a heaven was lost
> Seemed all unvalued and unknown...

Certainly she had humility; but he gives her other Christian virtues—

> So true she felt it that to *hope*,
> To *trust* is happier than to know.

But we may doubt if Tom knew what Bessy knew and excused. Sensibility will not dig very deep.

THE MAIDS

They tell me that a respectable and ancient profession, and one always honoured by literature, is dying out; and if that is true, then two more clauses of the tenth Commandment will lose their meaning. For a long time to come we shall go on grudging our neighbour his house—there's no doubt about that; but even as his ox and ass have ceased to enter into practical ethics because our average neighbour doesn't possess either, so we hear it is to be with his servant and his maid.

They have had their day. There are no domestic servants at the registries; the cap and apron, than which no uniform ever more enhanced a fair maid or extenuated a plain one, will be found only in the war museum, as relics of ante-bellum practice; we shall sluice our own doorsteps in the early morning hours, receive our own letters from the postman, have our own conversations with the butcher's young man at the area gate; and in time, perhaps, learn how it may be possible to eat a dinner which we have ourselves cooked and served up. Better for us, all that, it may well be; but will it be better for our girls? I am sure it will not.

Domestic service, I have said, is an employment which literature has always approved. From Gay to Hazlitt, from Swift to Dickens, there have been few writers of light touch upon life who have not had a kind eye for the housemaid. There's a passage somewhere in Stevenson for which I have spent an hour's vain hunting, which exactly hits the centre. The confidential relationship, the trim appearance, not without its suggestion of comic opera and the soubrette of the *Comédie Française*, the combined air of cheerfulness and respect which is demanded, mind you, on either side the bargain—all this is acutely and vivaciously observed in half a page by a writer who never missed a romantic opening in his days. The profession, indeed, has never lacked romance in real life. Strangeness has persistently followed beauty in and out of the kitchen. The number of old gentlemen who have married their cooks is really considerable. Younger gentlemen, whose god has been otherwhere, have married their housemaids. A Lord Viscount Townshend, who died in 1763 or thereabouts, did so in the nick of time, and left her fifty thousand pounds. Tom Coutts the banker, founder of the great house in the Strand, married his brother's nursemaid, and loved her faithfully for fifty years. She gave him three daughters who all married titles; but she was their ladyships' "dear Mamma" throughout; and Coutts himself saw to it that where he dined she dined also. There's nothing in caste in our country, given the essential solvent.

A stranger story still is this one. Some fifteen years ago a barrister in fair practice died, and made by will a handsome provision for his "beloved wife." This wife, thereby first revealed to an interested acquaintance, had acted as his parlourmaid for many years, standing behind his chair at dinner, and bringing him his evening letters on a tray; and she had been so engaged on the day of his death. Nobody of his circle except, of course, her fellow-servants, knew that she stood in any other relationship to her so-called master. I consider her conduct admirable; nor do I think his necessarily blameworthy. Those two, depend upon it, understood each other, and had worked out a common line of least resistance. On the distaff side there is the tale of the two maiden ladies so admirably served by their butler that when, to their consternation, he gave warning, they held a heart-to-heart talk together, as the result of which one of them proposed in all the forms to the invaluable man, and was accepted. It is deplorable that a pursuit which opens vistas so rose-coloured as these should be allowed to lapse.

A lady whom I knew well, and whose recent death I deplore, was cured of a bad attack of neuritis by being cut off all domestic assistance, except her cook's, and set to do her own housework. Therefore it is probable that we should all be the better for the same treatment; but, as I asked just now, will the girls be the better for it? The disengaged philosopher can only answer that question in one way. That feverish community-work which they have been doing through a four years' orgy of patriotism will have taught them very much of life and manners. It will have taught them, among other more desirable things, how to spend money, and how to keep a good many young men greatly entertained; but it will not, I fear, have taught them how to save money, how to make one man happy and comfortable, or how to bring up children in the fear of God.

And if it has failed to teach those things it will have failed to fit them for this world, to say the least. It will not only have failed them, but it will have failed us with them. For the world needs at this moment a thousand things before it can be made tolerable again; and all of those can be summed up into one paramount need, which is for men and women who will observe faithfully the laws of their being. And what, pray, are the laws of their being? At the outside, three; in reality, two: to work, to love and to have children.

At this hour neither men nor women will work. The strain is taken off, the bow relaxed. At the same time they must have money, that they may spend it; for as always happens in moments of reaction, the simplest way of expressing high spirits and a sense of ease is wild expenditure. So wages must be high, and because wages are high everything is dear. There are no houses, and there will be none; there can be no marriages, and there will be none; there will be no milk for children, so there will be no children. How long are such things to go on? Just so long as we disregard the laws of our being. We began to neglect them long before the war, and they must be learned again. We must learn first what they are, and next, how to keep them.

Now the education of men is another text; but for women there can be little doubt but that the prime educationary in the laws of being is domestic service. You can be ribald about it. That is easy. But where else is a girl to learn how to keep house? And if she does not learn how to be a mother, as indeed she may, poor dear, she gets to know very much of what to do when she becomes one.

So I hope to see a soberer generation of girls return to a profession which they have always adorned, for the schooling of which their husbands and children shall rise up and call them blessed.

POETRY AND THE MODE

A good friend of mine, poet and scholar, was recently approached by the President, or other kind of head of a Working Men's Association, for a paper. A party of them was to visit Oxford, where, after an inspection, there should be a feast, and after the feast, it was hoped, a paper from my friend— upon Addison. The occasion was not to be denied: I don't doubt that he was equal to it. I wish that I had heard him; I wish also that I had seen him; for he had determined on a happy way of illustrating and pointing his discourse. He had the notion of providing himself with a full-bottomed wig, a Ramillies; at the right moment he was to clothe the head of the President with it; and—Bless thee, Bottom, how art thou translated! In that woolly panoply, if one could not allow for *Cato* and the balanced antitheses of the grand manner, or condone rhetoric infinitely remote from life past, present or to come—well, one would never understand Addison, or forgive him. This, for instance:—

> CATO (*loq.*): Thus am I doubly arm'd; my death and life,
> My bane and antidote are both before me:
> *This* in a moment brings me to an end;
> But *this* informs me I shall never die.
> The soul, secured in her existence, smiles
> At the drawn dagger....

Ten pages more sententious and leisurely comment; then:

Oh! (*dies*).

There is much to be said for it, in a Ramillies wig. It is stately, it is dignified, it is perhaps noble. If, as I say, it is not very much like life, neither are you who enact it. But be sure that out of sight or remembrance of the wig such a tragedy were not to be endured.

That is very well. The wig serves its turn, inspiring what without it would be intolerable. I am sure my friend had no trouble in accounting for Addison in full dress and his learned sock. Nor need he have had with Addison the urbane, Addison of the *Spectator* condescending to Sir Roger de Coverley and Will Honeycomb. There is in that, the very best gentlemanly humour our literature possesses, nothing inconsistent with the full-bottomed wig and an elbow-chair. But when the right honourable gentleman set himself to compose *Rosamond: an Opera*, and disported himself thus:

PAGE:
Behold on yonder rising ground
The bower, that wanders
In meanders
Ever bending,
Never ending,
Glades on glades,
Shades in shades,
Running an eternal round.

QUEEN:
In such an endless maze I rove,
Lost in the labyrinths of love,
My breast with hoarded vengeance burns,
While fear and rage
With hope engage,
And rule my wav'ring soul by turns—

then I do not see how the wig can have been useful. I feel that Addison must have left it on the bedpost and tied up his bald pate in a tricky bandana after the fashion of Mr. Prior or Mr. Gay, one of whom, if I remember rightly, did not disdain to sit for his picture in that frolic guise. The wig, which adds age and ensures dignity, would have been out of place there; nor is it possible that *The Beggar's Opera* owes anything to it. To explain the Addison of *Rosamond* or *The Drummer*, my friend would have had to shave the head of his victim and clap a nightcap upon it.

The device was ingenious and happy. You yoke one art
to serve another. It can be extended in either direction,
working backwards from the Ramillies, or forwards, as I
propose to show. Skip for a moment the Restoration and
the perruque, skip the cropped polls of the Roundheads;
with this you are in full Charles I.

Go, lovely Rose!
Tell her that wastes her time and me,
That now she knows,
When I resemble her to thee,
How sweet and fair she seems to be.

What vision of what singer does that evoke? What other than that of a young gallant in a lace collar, with lovelocks over his shoulders, pointed

Vandyke fingers, possibly a peaked chin-beard? There is accomplishment enough, beauty enough, God knows; but there is impertinence too; it is *de haut en bas*—

Tell her that wastes her time and me!

Lovelocks and pointed fingers all over it. It is witty, but does not bite. If you bite you are serious, if you bite you are in love; but that is elegant make-believe. He will take himself off next minute, and encountering a friend, hear himself rallied:

> Quit, quit, for shame I This will not move,
> This cannot take her;
> If of herself she will not love,
> Nothing can her make:
> The D——l take her!

Laughter and a shrug are the end of it. With the Carolines it was not music that was the food of love, but love that was a staple food of music. A man who lets his hair down over his shoulders may be as sentimental as you please, or as impudent. He cannot nourish both a passion and a head of hair. He won't have time.

There, then, again, is a clear congruity established between your versifying and your clothes; they will both be in the mode, and the mode the same. One feels about the Cavalier fashion that it was not serious either one way or the other. It had not the Elizabethan swagger; it had not the Restoration cynicism; it had not the Augustan urbanity. Go back now to the Elizabethan, and avoiding Shakespeare as a law unto himself, which is the right of genius—for the sonnets have wit as well as passion (but a mordant wit), everything that real love-poetry must have, and much that no poetry but Shakespeare's could possibly survive—avoiding Shakespeare, I say, take two snatches in order. Take first—

> Thou art not fair, for all thy red and white,
> For all those rosy ornaments in thee,—
> Thou art not sweet, though made of mere delight,
> Nor fair nor sweet—unless thou pity me!

That first; and then this:

> Shake hands for ever, cancel all our vows
> And when we meet at any time again,
> Be it not seen in either of our brows
> That we one jot of former love retain—

and consider them for what they are: unapproachably beautiful, passionate, serious, on the edge of cynicism, but never over it. There you have the love of a young age of the world, when young men, hard hit, could be sharp-tongued, bitter, and often (though not in those two) too much in earnest not to be shameless. Agree with me, and see the men who sang and the women they sang of in preposterous stuffed and starched clothes which made them unapproachable except at the finger-tips, and yet burning so for each other that by words alone and the music in them they could rend all the buckram and whalebone and make such armour vain! You may see in Elizabethan dress a return to Art, as in Elizabethan poetry you see a return to Learning; but neither was designed to prevent a return to Nature; rather indeed to stimulate it. And so you come back to this:

> Take thou of me smooth pillows, sweetest bed,
> A chamber deaf of noise and blind of light,
> A rosy garland and a weary head ...

which is the perfectly-clothed utterance of an Elizabethan longing to be rid of his clothes.

I don't propose to linger over the perruque. The Restoration was a time of carnival when, if the men were overdressed, the ladies were underdressed; and the perruque was a part of the masquerade. In such a figurehead you could be as licentious as you chose—and you were; you could only be serious in satire. The perruque accounts for Dryden and his learned pomp, for Rochester and Sedley, and for Congreve, who told Voltaire that he desired to be considered as a gentleman rather than poet, and was with a shrug accepted on that valuation: it accounts for Timotheus crying Revenge, and not meaning it, or anything else except display; it accounts for Pepys thinking *King Lear* ridiculous. Let me go on rather to the day of the tie-wig, of Pope's Achilles and Diomede in powder; of Gray awaking the purple year; of Kitty beautiful and young, of Sir Plume and his clouded cane; of Mason and Horace Walpole. When ladies were painted, and their lovers in powder, poetry would be painted too. It would be either for the boudoir or the alcove. I don't call to mind a single genuine love-song in all that century among those who dressed *à la mode*. There were, however, some who did not so dress.

Gray was not one. Whether in the country churchyard, or by the grave of Horace Walpole's favourite cat, he never lost hold of himself, never let heart take whip and reins, never drowned the scholar in the poet, never, in fact, showed himself in his shirtsleeves. But before he was dead the hearts of men began to cry again. Forty years before Gray died Cowper was born;

fourteen years before he died, Blake was born; twelve years before he died, Burns. It is strange to contrast the *Elegy* with *The Poplar Field:*

> My fugitive years are all wasting away,
> And I must ere long be as lowly as they,
> With a turf on my breast and a stone at my head,
> Ere another such grove shall arise in its stead.

Put beside that melodious jingle the ordered diction and ordered sentiment of one of the best-known and most elegant poems in our tongue. They were written within fifteen years of each other. Within the same space of time, or near about it, there came this spontaneous utterance of simplicity, tragedy and hopeless sorrow:

> Young Jamie lo'ed me weel, and sought me for his bride;
> But saving a croun he had naething else beside:
> To make the croun a pund young Jamie gaed to sea;
> And the croun and the pund they were baith for me.

The authoress of that was born twenty-one years before Gray died. I speak, perhaps, only for myself when I say that reading that, or the like of that in Burns or in Blake, my heart becomes as water, and I feel that I would lose, if necessary, all of Milton, all of Shakespeare but a song or two, much of Dante and some of Homer, to be secured in them for ever. My friend (of the Ramillies) and I were disputing about a phrase I had applied to lyric poetry as the infallible test of its merit. I asked for "the lyric cry," and he scorned me. I could find a better phrase with time; but the quatrain just quoted makes it unmistakable, as I think. Anyhow, it will be conceded that there was some putting off of the tie-wig, the hoop and the red-heeled shoe about 1770.

In the time of Reform, say from 1795 to 1830, you could do much as you pleased, and dress according to your fancy. You could smother your neck in a stock, wear a high-waisted swallow-tail coat, kerseymere continuations and silk stockings. So sat Southey for his portrait, and so did Rogers continually. Or you could wear a curly *toupé* with Tom Moore and the Prince Regent, be as rough as a dalesman with Wordsworth or as sleek as a dissenting minister with Coleridge, an open-throated pirate with Byron, or a seraph with Shelley. If the rules lingered, they were relaxed. I think there were none. Individuality was in the air; schools were closing down. For the first time since the spacious days men sang as they pleased, and some sang as they felt and were, but with this difference added that you would no longer identify the age with the utterance. There were many survivals: most of Coleridge, all of Rogers, much of Byron, some of Wordsworth (*Laodamia*) is eighteenth century; and then, for the first time, you could archaicize or walk in Wardour Street—Macpherson had taught us that, and Bishop Percy. But all of Shelley and Keats, the best of Coleridge and Wordsworth belong to no age.

> The pale stars are gone!
> For the sun, their swift shepherd,
> To their folds them compelling,
> In the depths of the dawn,
> Hastes in meteor-eclipsing array and they flee
> Beyond his blue dwelling,
> As fawns flee the leopard.
> But where are ye?

That is like nothing on earth: music and diction are stark new. And that was the way of it for a forty years of freedom.

Then came a reaction. With Queen Victoria we all went to church again in our Sunday clothes. You cannot date Keats, Shelley and Wordsworth by the fashions; but you can date Tennyson assuredly. He belongs to the top-hat and the crinoline; to *Friends in Council* and "nice feelings." True, there was nothing dressy about Tennyson himself. I doubt if he ever wore a top-hat. But is not *The Gardener's Daughter* in ringlets? Did not Aunt Elizabeth and Sister Lilia wear crinolines? And as for *Maud*—

> Look, a horse at the door,
> And little King Charley snarling:
> Go back, my lord, across the moor,
> You are not her darling.

That settles it. "Little King Charley's" name would have been Gyp. I yield to no man in my admiration of *In Memoriam*; but when one compares it with *Adonais* it is impossible not to allocate the one and salute the other as for all time and place:

> When in the down I sink my head
> Sleep, Death's twin-brother, times my breath;
> Sleep, Death's twin-brother, knows not Death,
> Nor can I dream of thee as dead.

And then:

> He lives, he wakes—'tis Death is dead, not he;
> Mourn not for Adonais. Thou young Dawn,
> Turn all thy dew to splendour, for from thee
> The spirit thou lamentest is not gone.

No: *In Memoriam* is a beautiful poem, and technically a much better one than *Adonais*. But the spirit is different; narrower, more circumscribed; in a word, it dates, like the top-hat and the crinoline.

In our day, clothes have lost touch with mankind, they cover the body but do not express the soul. With the vogue of the short coat, short skirt, slouch hat, and brown boots, style has gone out and ease come in; and with ease, it would seem, easy, not to say free-and-easy, manners. I speak not of the "nineties" when a young degenerate could lightly say,

I have been faithful to thee, Cynara, in my fashion,

and be praised for it, but rather of the Georgians, of whom a golden lad, who happily lived long enough to do better, wrote thus of a lady of his love:

And I shall find some girl, perhaps,
And a better one than you,
With eyes as wise, but kindlier,
And lips as soft, but true.
And I daresay she will do.

If that is not slouch-hat and brown boots, I don't know what to call it. For that golden lad I think *The Shropshire Lad* must answer, who perhaps brought corduroys into the drawing-room. And if that is to be the way of it, we should do well to go back to Lovelace or Waller, and make believe with a difference. I shall find myself watching the sunny side of Bond Street for a revival—because while one does not ask for passion, or even object to the tart flavours of satiety, I feel that there is a standard somewhere, and a line to be drawn. Taste draws it. I trouble myself very little with the morals of the matter, yet must think manners very nearly half of the conduct of life. And the manners which are expressed in clothes are those which are instilled in art. They are symptomatic alike and correlated. There is nothing surprising about it, or even curious. It would be so, and it is so. If Milton had not on a prim white collar and a doctor's gown I misread *Paradise Lost* and *Lycidas* too.

POLYOLBION

How precisely does the Englishman love England? I remember saying some years ago that he was not patriotic in the ordinary sense, because though he loved the land, he had very little feeling for the political entity called England—whereas both will be loved by the true patriot. On recent consideration of the matter I am beginning to ask whether he does, after all, love the land itself, as the Irishman loves his, the Scot his, the Switzer his, and the Greek his. I must say that I doubt it. There is this, I think, to be noted of fervent patriots, that the object of their devotion will have had a distressful story. That is the case with the four nations just remarked upon. It has been the case with France ever since France was the passion of the French.

Every man loves his home, for reasons not necessarily connected with the country which happens to hold it; every one of our soldiers of late longed to get back, by no means necessarily because he wanted to see England again. Did he really want to see it at all—I mean for its own sake apart from what it held of his? I know that he would have cut his tongue out sooner than have confessed it. That is his nature, and I can't help liking him for it—because it is a part of himself, and I like him better than any man in the world. But allowing for that queer shyness, how are we to test his love of our country? Is there a sure test? Well, I know of one, which to my mind is a certainty. Judged by that I must own that Atkins does not stand as a lover should, or would.

My test is this. The lover of his countryside knows its physical features by heart, and to him they have personality. You will have observed the tendency of Londoners to guide you by the names of public-houses; you will have noticed their blank ignorance of points of the compass. To a great extent these defects characterise the Home Counties, and one might try to excuse them in various ways. In the North of England, and in Scotland throughout, you will be told to "go east," or "keep west" (as the Wordsworths were asked, were they "stepping westward?"), with a conviction that the direction will be sufficient for you as it plainly is for your guide. Now nobody can be said to know his countryside who does not know the airts; and the plain truth is that the Southern Englishman does not know his countryside at all. How, then, can he love it? But there's a stronger point than that.

Nothing is more surprising than the indifference of Southerners to their rivers. Where, for instance, throughout its course do you ever hear the Thames spoken of as "Thames" — as if it was a person, which no doubt it is? In the North you talk of Lune and Leven, Esk and Eden:

> Tweed said to Till,
> What gars ye run so still?

Scotland shows the same respect. Do you remember when Bailie Nicol Jarvie points out the Forth to Francis? "Yon's Forth," he said with great solemnity. That was well observed by Scott. In Italy — notably in Tuscany — a river is always spoken of without the definite article. It may be the case in Devonshire too; but it is never done here in South Wilts though we have five beautiful streams ministering to our county town. Indeed Wiltshire people are nearly as bad as the Cockneys, who always call their Thames "the river," which is as if a man might say "the railway."

Beautiful how Burns personified his rivers! More, he individualised them. The same verb won't do. You have:

Where Cart rins rowin' to the sea,

but

Where Doon rins wimplin' clear;

And Dante says, or makes Francesca say,

> Siede la terra dove nata fui
> Sulla marina dove Po discende
> Per aver pace co' seguaci sui.

Per aver pace: a lovely phrase. And that brings me to Michael Drayton.

That was a poet — author also of one lovely lyric — who treated our rivers after the fashion of his day, which ran to length and tedious excess. Shakespeare's *Venus and Adonis* is by pages too long; but that is nothing to Drayton's masterpiece. With the best dispositions in the world I have never been able to get right through the *Polyolbion*. His anthropomorphism is surprising, and a little of it only, amusing.

Here is an example, wherein he desires to express the fact that an island called Portholme stands in the Ouse at Huntingdon.

> Held on with this discourse, she—[that is, Ouse]—not so far hath run, But that she is arrived at goodly Huntingdon Where she no sooner views her darling and delight, Proud Portholme, but becomes so ravished with the sight, That she her limber arms lascivious doth throw About the islet's waist, who being embraced so, Her flowing bosom shows to the enamour'd Brook;

and so on.

That will be enough to show that one really might have too much of the kind of thing. In Drayton you very soon do; every page begins to crawl with demonstrative monsters, and there is soon a good deal more love-making than love. But you may read Drayton for all sorts of reasons and find some much better than others. He describes Britain league by league, and is said to have the accuracy of a roadbook. In thirty books, then, of perhaps 500 lines apiece, he conducts you from Land's End to Berwick-on-Tweed, naming every river and hill, dramatising, as it were, every convolution, contact and contour; and not forgetting history either. That means a mighty piece of work, of such a scope and purport that we may well grudge him the doing of it Charles Lamb, who loved a poet because he was bad, I believe, as a mother will love a crippled child, is more generous to Drayton than I can be. "That panegyrist of my native earth," he calls him, "who has gone over her soil, in his *Polyolbion*, with the fidelity of a herald, and the painful love of a son; who has not left a rivulet so narrow that it may be stept over, without honourable mention; and has animated hills and streams with life and passion beyond the dreams of old mythology." No more delightful task could be the lifework of a poet who loved his own land; but it could hardly be done again, nor, I dare say, ever be done again so well.

To describe, however, the windings and circumfluences of rivers, the embraces of mountain and rain-cloud in language on the other side of amorousness may easily be inconvenient or ridiculous, and not impossibly both; but I shouldn't at all mind upholding in public disputation, say, at the Poetry Bookshop, that there was no other way than Drayton's of doing the thing at all. It was the mythopoetic way. For purposes of poetry, Britain is an unwieldy subject, and if you are to allow to a river no other characters than those of mud and ooze, swiftness or slowness, why, you will relate of it little but its rise, length and fall. Drayton's weakness is that he can conceive of no other relation than a sex-relation, and in so describing the relations of every river in England, he very naturally becomes tedious. Satiety is the bane of the amorist, and of worse than he. Casanova had that in front of him when he set out to be immoral, *on ne peut plus*, in seven volumes octavo. There simply were not enough vices to go round. He ended, therefore, by being a dull as well as a dirty dog. "Take back your bonny Mrs. Behn," said Walter Scott's great-aunt to him after a short inspection, "and if you will take my advice, put her in the fire, for I found it impossible to get through the very first novel." The nemesis of the pornographer: he can't avoid boring you to tears.

THE WELTER

Soused still to the ears in the lees of war, I win a rueful reminder from a stray volume of *Hours in a Library*. Was the world regenerated between 1848 and 1855? Were English labourers all properly fed, housed and taught? Had the sanctity of domestic life acquired a new charm in the interval, and was the old quarrel between rich and poor definitely settled? Charles Kingsley (of whom the moralist was writing) seems really to have believed it, and attributed the exulting affirmative to—the Crimean War! The Crimean War, after our five years of colossal nightmare, looks to us like a bicker of gnats in a beam; yet perhaps any war will do for a text, since any war will produce some moral upheaval in the generations concerned. Let us suppose, then, that the British were seriously turned to domestic politics in 1855; let us admit that they are so turned to-day, and ask ourselves fairly whether we are now in a better way of reasonable living than history shows those poor devils to have been.

If we are, it will not be the fault of the old agencies, in which Kingsley always believed. Church and State are adrift; organised Christianity has abdicated; the aristocracy no longer governs even itself; Parliament has died of a surfeit of its own rules. If fundamental reform is to come, it will be forced upon us by the working class, and (at the pinch) opposed tooth and nail by the privileged. But is it to come? Is the working class deploying for action? In all the miscellaneous scrapping which we watch to-day is there one strong man with a sense of direction? It doesn't look like it.

Men, having learned to get what they lust after by strife, do not easily forget the lesson. Sporadic war, like a heath fire, breaks out daily in some part of the world; and society is as easily kindled, and as irrationally as nations. A Jew is put out of Hungary and an Archduke takes his place. The working men of Britain, having chosen a Parliament which they don't believe in, and didn't want, set to work, not to get rid of it, but to make any future Parliament impossible. The police do their best for the shoplifters; the engine-drivers, to help the police, prevent them from going home to bed. Sir Edward Carson, a staunch Unionist, makes union out of the question. The bakers, to improve the prospects of their trade, teach people to make their own bread. The colliers—well, the colliers do not yet seem to have found out that unless they provide people with coal, people won't provide them with many things they are in need of.

This doesn't look much like solidarity, it must be owned; and yet I make bold to say that the one abiding good we have got out of the war is the discovery of the solidarity of man. Nationality (mother of war) has been killed since we have learned from the Germans how much alike we are at our worst, and best. Caste is mortally wounded. The land-girl and her ladyship admit their sisterhood; the staff officer and the batman understand each other in the light of common needs and their satisfaction. There's the seed; water it with the dew of common poverty and you may have one Britain instead of a round dozen, and a League of Men to succeed a stillborn League of Nations. Courage, then; *Eppur si muove!*

Poverty is certainly coming, for Europe is on the edge of bankruptcy. With poverty will come freedom, and it can come in no other way. Nobody is free while he is serf to his own necessities, and the necessities of such a man as I am (to take the first instance that comes to hand) have grown to such a pitch that I am as rogue and peasant slave to them as ever Hamlet was to his. Gentleman born, quotha! Caste and self-indulgence go hand in hand. I must be a great man in the village, therefore live in the great house. Men must touch their hat-brims to me, therefore my hat (not I) must be worth their respect. A village girl must wait upon me, therefore (for my life) I must not wait upon her. That is where I have been ever since I was born, but now I am going to be poor and free. The time is at hand when I must give up my roomy old house in its seven-acre garden and live in the five-roomed cottage now occupied by my gardener. My hat must be as it may, since I shan't buy a new one. If a maid comes to work in my house she can only come in one capacity, which will equally involve my working in hers. She in the kitchen, I in the coalhole or potato patch, 'twill be all one. If she works it will be in our common interest; and for that I too shall work.

If I, still harping on myself, go that way to freedom, shredding off what is tiresome, cumbrous and a hindrance, one is tempted to think we shall all—so life is in a concatenation—lose what is really vicious in our social coil; and if in our social then in our political coil. For if the essence of a sound private life is that a man should be himself, so a public life for its smooth working depends upon the same sincerity. Read my parable of the particular into society at large. If I am to live so, and gain, are not nations? Are we to hire a great navy, a great army, to secure us in things which we have seen to be tiresome, cumbrous and a hindrance? Are we to exact flag-dippings from nations to our flag? Are we to make washpots of the Maltese, Cypriotes, Hindoos, Egyptians, Hottentots, and who not? If we go bankrupt we shall not be able to do it, and if we are not able to do it we shall stand among people as Britons, not as a British Empire, over against French, Germans, Maltese, Cypriotes, standing as their needs involve, and for what worth their virtue can ensure. So men, being men, nations of men will become families of men:

Magnus ab integro sæclorum nascitur ordo.

Two things therefore are clear: men are a family, and the family is to be poor. Almost as clear to me is the coming of the day when we shall slough the ragged skin of empire and become again a small, hardy, fishing and pastoral people. The profiteers will leave us, like rats and their parasites. We shall be able to feed ourselves by our industry. We shall be contented, and as happy as men with inordinate desires and subordinate capacities can ever hope to be. There is no reason to suppose that we need cease to be a nursery of heroes, that our old men will not see visions or our young men dream dreams. Neither vision nor dream will be the worse for having its bottom in truth.

CATNACHERY

Catnach was a dealer in ballads. His stock line was the murderer's confession, and his standard price half a crown. I don't know that there is a Catnach now, or a market for Catnachery, but people collect the old ones. You find them in county anthologies, with one of which "*The Kentish Garland*, Vol. II., edited by Julia H.L. de Voynes, Hertford: Stephen Austin and Sons, 1882," I lately spent a pleasant morning in a friend's house. I should have liked Volume I., though it could not by any possibility have contained worse matter. That is my only consolation for missing it, because there are bad things and bad things, and if a thing of literature is bad enough, it may well be as entertaining as the best. I have long felt that there was a future for *Half-hours with the Worst Authors*. It might prove a goldmine to a resolute editor, and I hope I am not betraying a friend when I say that one of mine has laid the footings of such a collection as may some day add lustre to his name.[A] If I don't mistake, I can put him on to a thing or two now which he will be glad of.

[Footnote A: He is here following Edward FitzGerald.]

Every bad ballad has its archetype in a good one, and all ballads of whatsoever quality, can be pigeonholed under subjects, whether of content or of treatment. My first specimen from Kent could be classified as the Ballad Encomiastic, or, at will, as the Ballad of Plain Statement, in which latter case it would be considered as a ballad proper and derive itself *passim* from Professor Child's book. In the former case you would have to go back to Homer for its original. It calls itself "An Epitaphe" — which it could not be — "uppon the death of the noble and famous Sir Thomas Scott of Scottshall, who dyed the 30 Dec. 1594," and begins thus:

> Here lyes Sir Thomas Scott by name —
> O happie Kempe that bore him!

> Kempe is his mother.

> Sir Reynold with four knights of fame
> Lyv'd lynealy before him.

The poet chooses to treat of ladies by their surnames, for we go on:

His wieves were Baker, Heyman, Beere,
His love to them unfayned;
He lived nyne and fiftie yeare.
And seventeen soules he gayned.

Seventeen children, in fact—but

His first wief bore them every one,
The world might not have myst her—

A very obscure line, at first blush rather hard on Baker, and flatly contradicted by what follows:

She was a very paragone,
The Lady Buckhurst's syster.

Nothing could be more succinct. Now for Beere:

His widow lives in sober sort,
No matron more discreeter;
She still reteines a good report,
And is a great housekeeper.

Apart from his valiancy as a consort Sir Thomas seems to have done little in the world but be rich in it. The best that can be said of him by the epigraphist is contained in what follows:

He made his porter shut his gate
To sycophants and briebors,
And ope it wide to great estates,
And also to his neighbours.

That does not recommend Sir Thomas to me. I suspect himself of sycophancy, if not of briebory, and it may well be that he shut out others of his kidney in order that he might have free play with the great estates. But that is not the poet's fault, who had to say what he could.

My next example should be styled the Ballad of Extravagant Grief, and will be found at its highest in the Poetical Works of John Donne. I can find nothing greater than his—

Death can find nothing after her, to kill
Except the world itself, so great as she,

in "A funerall elegie upon the death of George Sonds Esquire who was killed by his brother Mr. Freeman Sonds the 7 of August 1658." Freeman Sonds, a younger son, hit his brother George on the head with a cleaver as he lay in his bed, and thereafter dispatched him with a three-sided dagger.

He then went in to his father and confessed his fault. "Then you had best kill me too," said the father; to whom the son, "Sir, I have done enough." He was hanged at Maidstone, full of penitence and edifying discourse. The elegy begins in Donne's circumstantial manner:

> Reach me a handkerchief, another yet,
> And yet another, for the last is wet.

Nothing could be better; but he must needs outdo his usual outdoings, call for a bottle to hold his tears, finally require that—

> The Muses should be summoned in by force
> And spend their all upon the wounded corse—

which presents a rather comic picture to the imaginative reader.

The elegist, reserving blasphemy for his conclusion, now becomes foolish:

> In thy expyring it was made appear
> In bloody wounds the Trinity was here.

Where was the Trinity, you ask? In the wounds, naturally, which, made with a three-edged dagger, showed red triangles. But there were twelve wounds: therefore—

> The gates thro' which thy fertil soul did mount
> To blessed Aboad came to the full account
> Of Twelve, or four times three; and three
> Hath ever in it some great Mysterie.

Obviously. Here is his peroration:

> Great God, what can, what shall, man's frailtie thinke
> When thy great goodness at this act did winke?
> But thou art just, perhaps thou thoughtest it fit;
> And Lord, unto thy judgment I submit.

Any comment must fail upon the sublimity of that great "perhaps."

> Elkanah Settle might have written that, as he did
> undoubtedly another, "On the untimely death of Mrs.
> Annie Gray, who dyed of small pox":

> Scarce have I dry'd my cheeks but griefs invite
> Again my eyes to weep, my hand to write,
> Which still return with greater force, being more
> In weight and number than they were before.

A touch of Crabbe there—but enough of innocent death, which was not in Catnach's line of business. He dealt in murder, from the convicted murderer's standpoint. For us the *locus classicus* is the Thavies Inn Affair; but from the *Kentish Garland* I gather "The Dying Soldier in Maidstone Gaol," a later flower, written and published no longer ago than 1857.

The dying soldier was Dedea Redanies, so called, though probably his name should be spelt as it is rhymed, Redany. He was a Servian (not a Serbian) from Belgrade, engaged in the Second British-Swiss Legion, an armament of which I never heard before. Quartered at Shorncliffe, and goaded by jealousy, he stabbed his young woman, and her sister, on the cliffs above Dover, gave himself up, was tried and duly hanged. I hope that is a plain statement, but none which I could make could be plainer than Dedea's rhapsodist's:

> Oh, list my friends to a foreign soldier
> Whose name is Dedea Redanies—
> My friends and kindred had no idea
> That I should die on a foreign tree.
> I loved a maiden, a pretty maiden,
> In the town of Dover did she reside—
> I sweetly kissed her and with her sister
> I after killed and laid side by side.

That is admirably said, but not at all advantaged by subsequent re-statement in something like fifteen verses. The colossal egotism of the notorious criminal, however, provides him with a conclusion oleaginous enough for a scaremonger of our own day, with a confusion of *summject* and *ommject* very much after his heart. "O God," he whines—

> O God receive me, from pain relieve me,
> Since I on earth can no comfort find—
> To stand before thee, let me, in glory,
> With poor Maria and sweet Caroline.

I should like Sir Conan Doyle to treat of this modest proposal in a present lecture.

LANDNAMA

I have been reading in *Landnama Book* the records of the settlement of Iceland and can now realise how lately in our history it is that the world has become small. At the beginning of the last century it was roughly of the size which it had been at the end of the last millennium. It then took seven days to sail from Norway to Iceland, and if it was foggy, or blew hard, you were likely not to hit it off at all, but to fetch up at Cape Wharf in Greenland. It was some such accident, in fact, which discovered Iceland to the Norwegians. Gardhere was on a voyage to the Isle of Man "to get in the inheritance of his wife's father," by methods no doubt as summary as efficacious. But "as he was sailing through Pentland frith a gale broke his moorings and he was driven west into the sea." He made land in Iceland, and presently went home with a good report of it. He may have been the actual first discoverer, but he had rival claimants, as Columbus did after him. There was Naddodh the Viking, driven ashore from the Faroes. He called the island Snowland because he saw little else. Nevertheless, says his historian, "he praised the land much." Such was the beginning of colonisation in Thule. It was accidental, and took place in A.D. 871.

But those who intended to settle there had to devise a better way of reaching it than that of aiming at somewhere else and being caught in a storm. What should you do when you had no compass? One way, perhaps as good as any, was Floki Wilgerdsson's. "He made ready a great sacrifice and hallowed three ravens who were to tell him the way." It was a near thing though. The first raven flew back into the bows; the second went up into the air, but then came aboard again. "The third flew forth from the bows to the quarter where they found the land." It was then very cold. They saw a frith full of sea-ice—enough for Floki. He called the country Iceland, and the name has stuck. They stayed out the spring and summer, then sailed back to Norway, of divided minds concerning the adventure. "Floki spoke evil of the country; but Herolf told the best and the worst of it; and Thorolf said that butter dripped out of every blade of grass there." He was a poet and his figure clove to him. "Therefore he was called Butter Thorolf."

The first real settlers were two sworn brethren, Ingolf and Leif. They went because they had made their own country too hot to hold them, having in fact slain men in heaps. This had been on a lady's account, Helga daughter of Erne. They had gone a-warring with Earl Atle's three sons, and been very friendly until they made a feast afterwards for the young men. At that feast one of the Earl's sons "made a vow to get Helga, Erne's daughter, to wife, and to own no other woman." The vow was not liked by anybody; and it was not, perhaps, the most delicate way of putting it. Leif in particular "turned red," having a mind to her himself. These things led to battle, and the Earl's son was killed. Then the sworn brethren thought they had best go to Iceland, and they did; but Leif took Helga with him. They left their country for their country's good, and for their own good, too.

Having found your asylum, how did you choose the exact quarter in which to settle? The popular way was that adopted by the sworn brethren. "As soon as Ingolf saw land, he pitched his porch-pillars overboard to get an omen, saying as he did so, that he would settle where the pillars should come ashore." That was his plan. If it wasn't porch-pillars it was the pillars of your high seat. Either might be the nucleus of your house; both sets were sacred things, heirlooms, symbols of your worth. You never left them behind when you flitted. Another plan, and a good one, was to leave the site to Heaven. Thorolf, son of Ernolf Whaledriver, did that. He was a great sacrificer, and put his trust in Thor. He had Thor carven on his porch-pillars, and cast them overboard off Broadfrith, saying as he did so, "that Thor should go ashore where he wished Thorolf to settle." He vowed also to hallow the whole intake to Thor and call it after him. The porch-pillars went ashore upon a ness which is called Thorsness to this day, as the site of the shrine Thorolf built is still called Templestead. Thorolf was a very pious colonist. "He had so great faith in the mountain that stood upon the ness that he called it Holyfell;" and he gave out that no man should look upon it unwashed. It should be sanctuary also for man and beast, a hill of refuge. "It was the faith of Thorolf and all his kin that they should all die into this hill." I hope that they did so, but *Landnama Book* doesn't say.

There were few, if any, Christians among these fine people. King Olaf and his masterful ways with the heathen were yet to come. And those who took on the new religion took it lightly. They cast it, like an outer garment, over shoulders still snug in the livery of Frey and Thor. It was not allowed to interfere with their customs, which were free, or their manners, which were hearty. Glum, son of Thorkel, son of Kettle Black, "took Christendom when he was old. He was wont thus to pray before the Cross, 'Good for ever to the old! Good for ever to the young.'" That seems to have been all his prayer, which was comprehensive enough. But there are older and more obstinate garments than religions. Illugi the Red and Holm-Starri "exchanged lands and wives with all their stock." But the plan miscarried, for Sigrid, who was

Illugi's wife, "hanged herself in the Temple because she would not change husbands." The compliment was greater than Illugi deserved.

With the world as large as it was in those spacious days there was room for strange things to happen. Here is the experience of Grim, son of Ingiald. "He used to row out to fish in the winter with his thralls, and his son used to be with him. When the boy began to grow cold they wrapt him in a sealskin bag and pulled it up to his neck. Grim pulled up a merman. And when he came up Grim said, 'Do thou tell us our life and how long we shall live, or else thou shalt never see thy home again.' 'It is of little worth to you to know this,' he answered,' though it is to the boy in the sealskin bag, for thou shalt be dead ere the spring come, but thy son shall take up his abode and take land in settlement where thy mare Skalm shall lie down under the pack.' They got no more words out of him. But later in the winter Grim died, and he is buried there." So much for Grim. His widow took her son forth to Broadfrith, and all that summer Skalm never lay down. Next year they were on Borgfrith, "and Skalm went on till they came off the heath south to Borgfrith, where two red sand-dunes were, and there she lay down under the pack below the outermost sand-well." There the son of Grim set up his rest. There will nevermore be room in the world for things like that, but it is pleasant to know of them,

"WORKS AND DAYS"

Some time or another, Apollo my helper, I would choose to write a new *Works and Days* wherein the land-lore of our own Boeotia should be recorded and enshrined for a season. There should be less practice than Tusser gives you, less art than the *Georgics*, but rather more of each than Hesiod finds occasion for. Though it is long since I read the *Georgics*, I seem to remember that the poem was overloaded with spicy merchandise. You might die of it in aromatic pain. As for Tusser, certainly he is the complete Elizabethan farmer; sooner than leave anything out he will say it twice; sooner than say it twice, he will say it three times. Nevertheless he was a good farmer; as poet, his itch to be quaint and anxiety to find a rhyme combine to make him difficult. He writes like Old Moore:

> Strong yoke for a hog, with a twitcher and rings,
> With tar in a tarpot, for dangerous things;
> A sheep-mark, a tar-kettle, little or mitch,
> Two pottles of tar to a pottle of pitch.

"Mitch" is a desperate rhyme, but nothing to Tusser. He gives you a league or more of that; all the same, I don't doubt he was a better farmer than Virgil. More of him anon.

Hesiod also was a better farmer than Virgil, and a poet into the bargain, though the Mantuan had him there. He prefers terseness to eloquence, is on the dry side, and avoids ornament as if he was a Quaker. Such adjectives as he allows himself are Homer's, well-worn and familiar. The sea is *atrugetos*, Zeus *hypsibremetès*, the earth *polyboteirè*, the hawk *tanysipteros*, and so on. They have no more effect upon you than the egg-and-dart mouldings on your cornices. His own tropes are more curious than beautiful, but I cannot deny their charm. The spring, with him, is always *gray*—[Greek: polion ear]—which is exact for the moment when the breaking leaf-buds are no more than a mist over the woodlands. You shall begin your harvesting—

> When the House-carrier shuns the Pleiades,
> And climbs the stalks to get a little ease.

The House-carrier is the snail, of course; and he shuns the heat of the ground, not the Pleiades. Here again is a maxim deeply involved in language:

> When 'tis a god's high feast let not your knife
> Cut off the withered from the quick with life,
> Upon the five-brancht stock—

or, in other words, never cut your finger-nails on a holy day.

Hesiod, by birth an Æolian, was by settlement a Boeotian. He lived and farmed his own land on the slopes of Helikon, under the governance of the lords of Thespiæ, whoever they were. I have been to Thespiæ, and certify that there are no lords there now. I saw little but fleas and dogs of incredible savagery, where once were the precinct and shrine of Eros with a famous statue of the god by Praxiteles. It is not far from the Valley of the Muses, where or whereabouts those fair ladies met with Hesiod, and, as we are told in the Theogony, plucked him a rod of olive, a thing of wonder,

> And breath'd in me a voice divine and clear
> To sing the things that shall be, are, and were.

Also they told him to sing of the blessed gods,

> But ever of themselves both first and last,

and he obeyed them. When he won a tripod at Chalkis, in a singing contest, he dedicated it to his patronesses,

> There where they first instilled clear song in me.

So he was a grateful poet, which is very unusual.

In *Works and Days* he sang of what he knew best, the country round, and sang it as a poet should who was also a shrewd farmer and thrifty husbandman. It is full of the love of earth and of the ways of them who lie closest in her bosom; but it is full of the wisdom, too, which such men win from their mother, and are not at all unwilling to impart. There is a good deal of Polonius in Hesiod, who addresses his *Works and Days* to his brother Perses, a bad lot. Perses in fact had diddled him out of his patrimony, or part of it, by bribing the judges at Thespiæ; and the poet, who doesn't mince matters, loses no opportunity of telling him what he thinks of him. Indeed, one of Hesiod's reasons for instructing him in good farming was that thereby he might perhaps prevent him from spunging on his relations. So the injured bard got a sad, exalted pleasure out of his griefs, and something back, too, in his quiet way.

After a glance at the golden and other past ages he gets to work with a charming passage:

> Whenas the Pleiads, Atlas' daughters, rise
> Begin your harvest; when they hide their eyes,

> Then plow. For forty nights and forty days
> They are shrouded; then, as the year rounds, they raise
> Their shining heads what time unto the stone
> You lay your sickle's edge—

and that is your time for harvesting. But you must work hard; for the law of the plains, of the seaboard, and of the upland dales is the same:

> You who Demeter's gifts will win good cheap
> Strip you to plow and sow, and strip to reap—

and if you in particular, Perses, will do that, perhaps you won't need to go begging at other men's houses as you have begged at Hesiod's. But he gives you warning that you will get no more out of him—than advice.

The Pleiades, however, don't set till November, and before that there is October to be considered, the season of the rains. Get you into the woods in October and cut for your needs. And what might these be? Well, a mortar to pound your grain in, and a pestle to pound it withal; an axle for your wain, a beetle to break the clods. Then, for your plows, look out for a plow-tree of holm-oak: that is the best wood for them. Make two plows in case of accident, one all of a piece ([Greek: autogyon]), one jointed and dowelled. The pole should be of laurel or elm; the share must be oak. The [Greek: guês] is the plow-tree, and it is not always easy to find one ready-made—but get one if you can.

> Two oxen then, each one a nine year bull,
> Whose strength is not yet spent, the best to pull,
> Which will not fight i' the furrow, break the plow
> And leave your work undone. To drive them now
> Get a smart man of forty, fed to rights
> With a four-quartered loaf of eight full bites:
> That's one to work, and drive the furrow plim,
> Too old to gape at mates, or mates at him.

That precise loaf, with just that much bitage, is the staple in Boeotia to-day; but the [Greek: aizêos] of forty will not so readily be found. Elsewhere in his poem Hesiod recommends something more in accord with modern practice:

> Your house, your ox, your woman you must have;
> For she must drive the plow—not wife but slave.

The terms are synonymous in Greece to-day.

Plowing time is when you hear the crane in the clouds overhead. Be beforehand with your cattle.

When year by year high in the clouds the crane
Calls in the plow-time and the month of rain,
Take care to feed your oxen in the byre;
For easy 'tis to beg, but hard to hire.

That is in Tusser's vein, and no doubt comes naturally to rustic aphorists. A man may plow in the spring, too; and if Zeus should happen to send rain on the third day, after the cuckoo's first call, "As much as hides an ox-hoof, and no more," he may do as well as the autumn-tiller. In any case don't forget your prayers when you begin plowing:

You who in hand first the plow-handles feel,
Or on the ox's flank lay the first weal,
Pray Chthonian Zeus and chaste Demeter bless
The grain you sow with heart and heaviness.

Now for your vines. First, for the pruning, note this:

When, from the solstice sixty days being fled,
Arcturus leaves the holy Ocean's bed
And, shining, burns the twilight; when that shrill
Child of Pandion opens first her bill—
Before she twitters, prune your vines! 'Tis best.

No reasons at all: simply "[Greek: ôs gar ameinon]." That is like Homer. The stars continue their signals. Vintage time is when Orion and Sirius are come to mid-heaven, and rosy-fingered Dawn sees Arcturus. Then—

Cut your grape clusters off and bring to hive;
Show ten days to the sun, ten nights; for five
Cover them up; the sixth day draw all off—

That is the way of it, Perses, and much profit to you in my learning, you scamp.

Scattered up and down these frosty but kindly old pages are scraps of wisdom on all kinds of subjects—for life is Hesiod's theme as well as agriculture. He will tell you under what star to go to sea, if sail you must; but better not seafare at all. However, if you will go, choose fifty days after the summer solstice. That is the right time, the only pretty swim-time. If you must venture out in the spring, let it be when you see leaves on the fig-tree top as large as the print of a crow's foot—but even so the thing is desperate.

For me, I praise it not, nor like at all—
'Tis a snatcht thing—mischief is bound to fall.

Then there's marriage, certainly the greatest venture of all. Don't think of it until you are rising thirty, anyhow. And as for *her*:

> Let her be four years woman, and no more;
> In her fifth year take her, and shut the door
> Till she is yours, enured to your good laws.
> Take her from near at hand and give no cause
> That neighbours find your wedding stuff for mirth:
> Than a good wife no better thing on earth;
> Than a bad one, what worse? Pot of desire,
> That roasts her husband up without a fire!

That would make her sixteen or thereabouts. Poor child! But neither Homer, nor Hesiod, nor any Greek I ever read had any mercy on women. Hesiod in more than one page lets you know what he thinks about them. It comes hardly from one who in the *Eoioe*(if those apostrophes are his) was to hymn the great women of history and myth; but there, I think, spoke the courtier Hesiod, and not the husbandman.

Lastly come a mort of things which you must not do. Here are some— for some must be omitted from the decorous page:

> Let not your twelve-year-old presume to sit
> On things not to be moved. That's bad. His wit
> Will never harden; nor let a twelve-month child.
> Let no man wash in water that's defiled
> By women washing in it. Bitter price
> You pay for that in time. Burnt sacrifice
> Mock not, lest Heaven be angry … So do you
> That men talk not against you. Talk's a brew
> Mischievous, heady, easy raised, whose sting
> Is ill to bear, and not by physicking
> Voided. Talk never dies once set a-working—
> Indeed, in talk a kind of god is lurking.

I regret to record the manner of death of the mainly pleasant old country poet, still more the supposed cause of it—but it may not be true. The Oracle at Delphi, which it seems he consulted after his triumph at Chalkis, warned him that he would come by his end in the grove of Nemean Zeus. He took pains, therefore, to avoid Nemea in his travels, and chose to stay for a while at OEnoë in Lokris, "where," says Mr. Evelyn-White, his editor in the *Loeb Library*, "he was entertained by Amphiphanes and Ganyktor, sons of Phegeus." But you never knew when the Oracle would have you, or where. OEnoë was also sacred to Nemean Zeus, "and the poet, suspected by his hosts of having seduced their sister, was murdered there. His body, cast into the sea, was brought to shore by dolphins, and buried at OEnoë; at a later date his bones were removed to Orchomenos." An unhappy ending for the instructor of Perses! But it may not be true. To be sure, these poets—I can only say that to me it sounds improbable, and so, I take it, it sounded to Alkæus of Messene, who wrote this epigram upon his dust:

> When, in the Lokrian grove dead Hesiod lay,
> The Nymphs with water washt the stains away.
> From their own well they fetcht it, and heapt high
> The Mound. Then certain goatherds, being by,
> Poured milk and yellow honey on the grave,
> Minding the Muses' honey which he gave
> Living, that old man stored with poesy.

That, surely, bespeaks a happier end to Hesiod. It is an epitaph that any poet might desire.

THE ENGLISH HESIOD

Now for Tusser, whom I feel that I belittled in the last Essay in order to make a point for the Boeotian.

"Five Hundreth Points of Good Husbandry United to as Many of Good Huswifery" was the sixth edition in twenty years of a book which that fact alone proves to have been a power in its day. It was indeed more lasting than that, for it had twenty editions between 1557, when it began with a modest "Hundreth Pointes," and 1692, when the black-letter quartos ended. Thomas Tusser, the author of it, was a gentleman-farmer and had the education of one. He began as a singing-boy at Wallingford, went next to St. Paul's, then to Eton, where Nicholas Udall gave him once fifty-three strokes, "for fault but small or none at all"; presently to Cambridge, where Trinity Hall had him at nurse. All that done, he settled as a farmer under the Lord Paget in Suffolk; and there it was that in 1557 he published his notable book. Taking the months *seriatim*, beginning, as he should, in September, he runs through the whole round of work with an exhaustiveness and accuracy which could hardly be bettered to-day. Given a holding of the sort he had, a man might do much worse than obey old Tusser from point to point.

He wrote in verse, a verse which is not often much better than those rustic runes which still survive, wherein weather-lore and suchlike sometimes prompt and sometimes are prompted by a rhyme. The best of these semi-proverbial maxims are recalled by the best of Tusser. Take this of the autumn winds as an example:

> The West, as a father, all goodness doth bring,
> The East, a forbearer, no manner of thing;
> The South, as unkind, draweth sickness too near,
> The North, as a friend, maketh all again clear.

But he can be more pointed than that and no less just—as when he is telling the maids how to wash linen:

"Go wash well," saith Summer, "with sun I shall dry."
"Go wring well," saith Winter, "with wind so shall I."

He is never dull if he is never eloquent; he is always wise if he is seldom witty. Among the Elizabethan poets there will have been many of a lowlier quality, many who could not have reached the piety and sweet humour of "My friend if cause doth wrest thee," which, with its happy close of "And sit down, Robin, and rest thee," is the best known of all his rhymes. As a verbal acrobat I don't suppose any of them could approach him. His greatest feat in that kind was his "Brief Conclusion" in twelve lines, every word in every line of which began with T. Thus:

The thrifty that teacheth the thriving to thrive,
Teach timely to traverse the thing that thou 'trive,

and so on. If *Peter Piper* dates so early, Tusser beats it handsomely.

For the rest, he writes doggerel, and has no other pretensions that I can see. All the Elizabethans did, Shakespeare among the best of them. And I don't know that Shakespeare's doggerel is much better than Tusser's doggerel. It is something that, swimming in such a brave company, he should keep his head above water; and something more that in one other point Tusser can vie with the foremost. His knack of christening his personages with *ad hoc* names recalls Shakespeare's, which, with its Dick the Carter and Marian's nose, was of the same kind and degree. Here is an example, where he wishes to instil the value of hedge-mending. If you let your fences down, he says:

At noon, if it bloweth, at night if it shine,
Out trudgeth Hew Makeshift with hook and with line;
While Gillet his blowse is a milking thy cow,
Sir Hew is a rigging thy gate, or thy plow.

Autolycus sang like that. Now take an allusive couplet addressed to the house-mistress, that she by all means see the lights out:

Fear candle in hay-loft, in barn, and in shed,
Fear Flea-smock and Mend-breech for burning their bed.

Right Shakespearian direction: few words and to the mark. But Tusser is seldom up to that level, and never on it long.

We may as well be clear about the kind of farmer Tusser was before we go any further. A farmer, indeed, he happens to have been; but he was also a husbandman. A farmer in his day was a man who paid a yearly rent for something, by no means necessarily land. To farm a thing was to pay a rent for it. You could farm the tithe, or the King's taxes; you could farm a landlord's rent-roll, a corporation's market-dues, the profits of a bridge or of a highway. The first farmers of land were the men who took over all the estates of a monastery, paying the holy men a sufficiency, and making what they could over and above. In Elizabeth's time the great landlords had taken a leaf out of the monks' book, and the farmer of land was becoming more common. There were yet, however, many husbandmen who were not farmers at all: yeomen of soccage tenure, and tenants by copy of court-roll. That class was probably the most numerous of all, and Tusser, though he objected to its common fields, or "champion land," as he calls it, had plenty to tell them. He must, I think, himself have been a copyholder in his day, so feelingly does he deal with the detriments of a champion-holding. The need, for example, of watching the beasts straying at will over the open fields!

> Where champion wanteth a swineherd for hog
> There many complaineth of naughty man's dog.
> Where each his own keeper appoints without care,
> There corn is destroyed ere men be aware

And again more bitterly:

> Some pester the commons with jades and with geese,
> With hog without ring, and with sheep without fleece.
> Some lose a day's labour with seeking their own,
> Some meet with a booty they would not have known.
> Great troubles and losses the champion sees,
> And even in brawling, as wasps among bees:
> As charity that way appeareth but small;
> So less be their winnings, or nothing at all.

The probabilities are that he was quite right; but so long as copyhold endured so long lasted the open fields.

Tusser's holding, and that of every husbandman in England in his time, was self-sufficient. Not only did you eat your own mutton, make your own souse, your own beer, cheese, butter, wine, cordials, and physic; you built your own house, made your own roads, fenced your own lands, contrived your own plows, wains, wagons, wheelbarrows, and all manner of tools. But much more than that. You grew your own hemp, had your own ropewalk, twisted your own twine; you grew your flax and wove your linen; you tanned and dressed your own leather, cut and spun your own wool, made, no doubt, your own clothes. Indeed, you stood four-square to fate in Tusser's time; and in that particular, as well as in another which I must speak of next, you were much nearer to Hesiod's farmer than to ours. This precept of his upon the uses of your woodland recalls Hesiod directly:

> Save elm, ash and crabtree for cart and for plow;
> Save step for a stile of the crotch of the bough;
> Save hazel for forks, save sallow for rake;
> Save hulver and thorn, whereof flail to make.

Hulver is holly. In the same section (April) he has a verse about stone-picking which will show his encyclopædic grip of his matter:

> Where stones be too many, annoying thy land,
> Make servant come home with a stone in his hand:
> By daily so doing, have plenty ye shall,
> Both handsome for paving and good for a wall.

He bought little or nothing, trafficked very much by barter, and had scarcely any need for money. His men and maids lived in the house, and if they were paid anything, he does not say so. I suppose they were paid something, those of them who were not apprentices, bound for a seven years' term. They stood to his wife and himself as children, had their keep, learned their business, married each other by and by, and probably set up for themselves with a pig and a cock and hen on a pightle of land of the master's. It was a family relationship well into the eighteenth century. Horace Walpole used to call his servants his family. With the privilege of parenthood went the power of the rod. There's no doubt about that: maid and man had it if it was earned. In his dairy instruction Tusser gives us a list of "ten topping guests unsent for," whose presence in the cheese will cause Cicely to rue it. There are:

> Gehazi, Lot's wife, and Argus his eyes,
> Tom Piper, poor Cobler, and Lazarus's thighs:
> Rough Esau, with Maudlin, and gentles that scrawl,
> With Bishop that burneth—ye thus know them all.

Gehazi the leper is in cheese when it is white and dry; Lot's wife when it is too salt; Argus's eyes are obvious:

> Tom Piper hath hoven and puffed up cheeks;

poor Cobler is there when it is leathery; Esau betrays himself by hairs, Maudlin by weeping; and as for the "Bishop that burneth" the explanation is complicated. It seems that Cicely would run after the bishop for his blessing, and leave the milk on the fire to burn.[A] For all these ill-timed guests you are to baste Cicely, or "tug her a crash," or "make her seek creeks"; you "call her a slut," or "dress her down." But you encourage her at the end with this quatrain:

> "If thou, so oft beaten,
> Amendest by this,
> I will no more threaten,
> I promise thee, Cis."

[Footnote A: A correspondent from Yorkshire gives me a better explanation. In that county burnt milk is still said to be "bishoped." The bishop's power of the keys is thought to be hinted.]

Fizgig, too, which is his lively name for the kitchen knave, gets the holly-wand across his quarters when he deserves it; but Tusser seems to feel that discipline may be overdone. It may be waste of good stick and good pains, for:

> As rod little mendeth where manners be spilt,
> So naught will be naught, say and do what thou wilt;

and he is careful to remind you in concluding his chapter of Huswifely Admonitions that you had always better smile than scold:

> Much brawling with servant, what man can abide?
> Pay home when thou fightest, but love not to chide.

The whole matter of servants is amusing or rueful study nowadays, accordingly as one looks at servants. Their treatment under Tusser's handling brings the husbandman poet very near to Hesiod, in whose time servitude was not called by any other name. Tusser's huswife, warned by the matin cock, called up her maids and men at four in the summer, at five in the winter. She packed them off to bed at ten or nine at night, according to the season, and, it would appear, to bed in the dark. She made her own candles, and feared also a fire, which will account for that. There was no early tea for Mistress Tusser's maids, let me tell you:

> Some slovens from sleeping no sooner get up
> But hand is in aumbry and nose is in cup.

Nothing of the kind with Mrs. Tusser. On the other hand, hard work all round: "Sluts' corner" to be ridded; sweeping, dusting, mop-twirling,

> Let some to peel hemp, or else rushes to twine,
> To spin or to card, to seething of brine;

and as for the men:

> Let some about cattle, some pastures to view,
> Some malt to be grinding against ye do brew.

And so to breakfast. The morning star was the signal for it; and a hasty meal was expected of you:

> Call servants to breakfast, by day-star appear,
> A snatch, and to work—fellows tarry not here.

You had porridge and a scrap of meat, and if you laid hands on something sweeter, look out for Mrs. Tusser:

> "What tack in a pudding?" saith greedy gut-wringer:
> Give such ye wot what, ere a pudding he finger.

And, summarily, of breakfast there is this to be understood, that it is a thing of grace, not of custom:

> No breakfast of custom provide for to save,
> But only for such as deserveth to have.

Very near Hesiod indeed!

For your dinner at noon you were more hospitably served. First of all, it was ready for you:

> By noon see your dinner be ready and neat:
> Let meat tarry servant not servant his meat.

And you were to have enough—plain fare, but enough.

> Give servants no dainties, but give them enow;
> Too many chaps wagging do beggar the plow;

but even here you would get according to your deserts. If you were lazy at your threshing, you would be given a "flap and a trap," whatever those may be. And you were expected to eat the trencher bare:

> Some gnaweth and leaveth, some crusts and some crumbs:
> Eat such their own leavings, or gnaw their own thumbs.

In the hot weather you had time for sleep allowed you:

> From May to mid-August an hour or two
> Let Patch sleep a snatch, howsoever ye do.
> Though sleeping one hour refresheth his song
> Yet trust not Hob Grouthead for sleeping too long.

Then came afternoon work, and at last supper. Here the mistress might unbend somewhat; for, as Tusser puts it:

Whatever God sendeth, be merry withal.

She had still, however, an eye for the servants:

> No servant at table use sauc'ly to talk,
> Lest tongue set at large out of measure do walk;
> No lurching, no snatching, no striving at all,
> Lest one go without, and another have all.

And then a final word:

> Declare after supper—take heed thereunto—
> What work in the morning each servant shall do.

And then—bed!

There were feast days, of course: Christmas to Epiphany was one long feast; then Plow Monday, Shrovetide, Sheep-shearing, Wake-Day, Harvest Home, Seed-Cake—these as the times came round. But there was a weekly regale too, which was known as Twice-a-Week-Roast. On Sundays and Thursdays a hot joint was the custom at supper. Tusser is clear about the value and sanction at once:

> Thus doing and keeping such custom and guise,
> They call thee good huswife—they love thee likewise.

Those days are past and done, with much to regret and much to be thankful for. You trained good servants that way—but did you make good men and women? Some think so, and I among them; but such training is two-edged, and while I feel sure that the girls and lads were the better for the discipline, I cannot believe that the masters and mistresses were. They nursed arrogance; out of them came the tyrants and gang-drivers of the eighteenth century, Act of Settlement, the Enclosure Acts, Speenhamland, rick-burning, machine-breaking, and the Bloody Assize of 1831. Well, now the reckoning has come, and Hodge will have Farmer Blackacre at his discretion.

One or two variations from modern practice may be noted. The Elizabethan husbandman grew, I have said, his own flax and hemp; he grew his vines too, and Tusser bids him prune them in February. I, who grow mine, call that full early. He does not tell us when he gathered his grapes or (what I very much want to know) how he made his wine—whether with pure fermented grape-juice, which is the French way, or by adding water and sugar to the must, which is our present English fashion. Again, he used sheep's milk both for draught and for butter-making. I wish we had sheep's milk butter. No one who has had it in Greece would be without it at home if he could help it. You weaned the lambs at Philip and Jacob, he says, if you wanted any milk from the ewe. Lastly, he grew saffron, which he pared between the two St. Mary's days. To pare is to strip the soil with a breast-plow. The two St. Mary's days were July 22 and August 15, which would be a pretty good time to plant saffron.

We also, in my country, date our operations by holy days, long after the holy men have ceased to be commemorated. Who knows St. Gregory's Day? It is March 12. Marrowfat peas go into the drill:

> Sow runcivals timely, and all that is grey;
> But sow not the white till St. Gregory's Day.

I will undertake that half a dozen old hands round about my house follow out this rule in its entirety.

FLOWER OF THE FIELD

A county inquiry took me, one day last summer, deeply into the Plain, up and over a rutty track which my driver will have cause to remember. An uncommonly large hawk soaring over his prey, and so near the ground that I could see the light through his ragged plumes, a hare limping through the bents, further off a crawling flock bustling after shepherd and dog, were all the living things I saw. The ground was iron, the colour of what had once been herbage a glaring brown. Of the flowers none but the hardiest had outlived the visitation of the sun. I saw rest-harrow which has a root like whipcord, and the flat thistle which thrives in dust. The harebells floated no more, the discs of the scabious were shrivelled husks; ladies' bedstraw was straw indeed, but not for ladies' uses. Three miles away from anywhere we came upon a clump of dusty sycamores whose leaves were spotted and beginning to fall; beyond them was a squat row of flint and brick bungalows, the goal of our quest. There were three tenements, of which two were empty. In the third lives the shepherd who had called me up to consider his circumstances.

There was thunder about, though not visibly; a day both airless and pitiless; one of those days when you feel that the unseen powers are conspiring against your peace. A naked sun from a naked sky stared down upon a naked earth. It seemed to me that the hawk had been a figure of more than himself and his purpose; I saw him as Homer's people saw their eagles. Just as he hung aloft so hung the sun, intent upon the life of our cowering ball. Not elsewhere in England have I seen so shadeless a place, or one so unfitted for human intercourse, so lacking in the comfort, which human sensibilities need. We live in nature as hunted things, beasts of chase. Every eye is upon us in fear or dislike; but in our turn, cursed as well as blessed by imagination, we people the wild with dreadful shapes of menace. The heat, the cold, the wind and the rain work as much against us as for us. We endow them with minds like our own, but magnified by our dismay to be the minds of gods maleficent. Without shelter of our own provision we are comfortless, and without comfort our souls perish, then our bodies. Salisbury Plain, swooning in the heat, is a paradise for insects. In those desolate dwellings both flies and (I am sure) fleas abounded, dreadfully healthy and alive. I only guess at the fleas, but the flies I can answer for.

They swarmed on the baking walls and wove webs in the air above us. The rooms were black with them, and their humming filled them up with noise.

Here lived the shepherd, too heavily taxed as he thought for his hermitage; here lived his family of half a dozen swarthy and beautiful children; and here we discussed the state of affairs, since the shepherd was abroad, with his daughter, a flower of the field. She came out of this stivy tenement at the sound of our boiling radiator, and stood framed in the doorway, shading her eyes against the sun, a tall and graceful, very pretty girl, dressed in cool white which might have been fresh from its cardboard box, as she herself might have stepped from her typewriter and Government office at Whitehall. Gentle-voiced, quiet and self-possessed, she showed us the conditions of her lot. One living-room, two bedrooms, and a washhouse in a shed: three miles over the grass to shop, church, post-office, and doctor; half a mile to call up a neighbour in case of need. A rain-water tank, less than a quarter full of last winter's rain, must keep clean her house and her, and for drinking she was served by a galvanised tank in full sun, which she was lucky to get filled once a week.

I tasted of it. The water was warm, flat, and not too clean. "Where does this come from?" "It is fetched in a barrel from over the hill." "Who brings it?" "The farmer—but he makes a fuss whenever we ask for it." "He must water the stock, surely?" "Oh yes, and the sheep, too, but—" A pregnant aposiopesis. I wondered if that tank could not be put in the shade; but it seemed that it could not. The water had to be drawn from the barrel, the barrel was on wheels; time was short, life was tough; and so—you see! We did justice to the shepherd.

It is shocking that a man should live so, held of less account than the sheep which he rears; but it is admirable that this man should live as he does. The house, to call it so, was as clean as a dairy; the children were neat, washed and brushed; the girl was one for Herrick to have sung of. I wish that I could have seen the shepherd, though it may well be that his wife, if she is alive, would reveal more. Something told me that he was a widower, and that this fair young woman mothered his brood for him. What she had of the nest-lore can only have come from a shrewd mistress of it. I did not see a book in the place, nor a newspaper.

Life out there, on such terms, is more solitary than in Northumberland, where the farms are isolated and self-sufficient, but all the hinds' dwellings are clustered, and society may be had. I don't believe you can set up for a successful hermit without a long education; and although a shepherd himself may be one by a stern schooling in solitude, you should not expect it of his daughter. Here was a girl made for social amenity, who would want to be danced with, flirted with, courted with flowers, sweets and other delicate observance. She deserved admiration both to receive and impart. It is useless to talk about nature; the love of that is both sophisticated and acquired. Nothing to her the great blue spaces of the Plain, the brooded mystery of Stonehenge, the companionship of her long-dead ancestry, dust in their barrows. No solace for her, after the burden of the day, in the large solemnity of evening out there, which to some of us would call a message almost vocal. To me, for instance, a summer's dusk, a moonrise on the Plain, are poems without words. Heard melodies are sweet, but those unheard—!

For whom, then, had she adorned herself in white raiment, for whom dressed her dark hair? Not for us, that's certain. She had had no notice of our coming. That she should do such things for their own sake, *elegantiâ quadam prope divinum,* was original virtue in her. Solomon in all his glory had been no goodlier sight; and if she toiled or spun to achieve it, her state, I should say, is by so much the more gracious. And what the devil does she do with herself in the long winter nights, when you light the lamp at four and see nothing of the sun till eight the next morning—and she arrayed like a lily of the field? There's mending, but you have the afternoon for that; a letter to a brother in Canada; let us hope there's one to a sweetheart not so far away. And then—what? To-morrow, and to-morrow, and to-morrow.

UNDER THE HARVEST MOON

She is at her full, and even as I write rising red and heavy in the south-west. All night long she will look down upon at least one corner of the earth satiate with the good things of life. I don't remember such a September as this has been for many years past. Misty, gossamered mornings, a day all blue and pale gold, bees in the ivy bloom, sprawling overblown flowers, red apples, purpling vine-clusters, clear evenings: then this smouldering moon to go to bed by! It is all like a great Veronese wall-picture, or the Masque in *The Tempest*—"Rich scarf to my proud earth!"—and summons from me more adjectives than I have needed this twelvemonth. It is indeed adjectival weather; for Nature is still adding, not discarding stores. The last act of the "maturing sun" is to ingerminate the flowers and fruit which will bless or tantalise us next year.

Now is the time when maids get up at six and hunt for mushrooms in the dew; now the good wives of the village make wine of all sorts of unlikely fruits, blackberries, elderberries, peaches, pears, and, of all things in the world, parsnips. I have lately been given of this wine to taste. It is a cordial rather than a wine and on the good rather than the bad side. The addition of spices is admitted; nevertheless out of a particularly mawkish vegetable is made a palatable drink. "Out of the strong come forth sweetness." After it I shall be prepared to find a potable in the banana, which is favoured by many people, of whom I am not one. But I don't find it nastier than the parsnip, and it is evident that fermentation can work miracles.

In such a year as this I, too, shall have a vintage. For the first time in my life I shall tread my own winepress, vat my own must, and (I hope) need no sugar for it. I don't know why it is, but I can conceive no more romantic rural adventure than that of growing and drinking your own wine. But there are yet many things to happen. The grapes must get ripe and the wasps be kept off; and then there are problems connected with vinification which I have not yet solved. The Marquis of Bute could tell me all about it, and I wish he would. He has made wine at Castle Coch these many years, and of the most excellent. Unfortunately I have not his acquaintance, so I invite advice, and shall be grateful for it. The chief of my perplexities are concerned with the beginning of fermentation and the end of it. For the first, should I use yeast? My neighbours here say, yes; the French tell me that I don't need it, the grapes having enough of their own. Pass that and consider the second point. Having started your ferment, how do you stop it?[A] Fermentation in Italy goes on in the barrel, after the liquor has left the vat. That gives you a peculiar prickly wine which the Italians call "Frizzante" and profess to like. Our word for it is "beastly."

> [Footnote A: Since that was written I have learned the answer. It stops itself—why, I don't know, unless by the grace of God.]

My village gossips tell me that fermentation will stop of itself when I draw the wine off the lye; but the French practice certainly seems to be to burn sulphur matches in the vat and so kill the vinegar germs there latent. And then *plâtrage*? You sprinkle the must with plaster of Paris before fermentation begins. Is that done in England? It is not done in this part of England at least. Nor do I know why it is done in France. Probably before I have solved my problems by stomach-ache and other experiences of a biliary kind, prohibition will be in the air over here, wafted upon some newspaper breeze from America. There will be no difficulty in starting a fermentation out of that sweeping doctrine, that's for certain. I don't say that we need take prohibition seriously; but we think about it, naturally, and talk about it out here.

If it were put to the local vote in this village, it would be lost. We have many total abstainers, yet one of them, I know, and several of them, I believe, would vote against it. Says the one I am sure of: "If I abstain from strong drink, as I do, it is my own doing; and if I were tempted to a fall and withstood it, that is to my credit. But if the law cuts me off it, and I am a criminal if I drink, it cuts me off a good part of my credit too—and I am against that." My friend has there put his finger upon a sharp little dilemma. If alcohol is a bad thing, then prohibition is a good thing. But if temperance is a good thing, then prohibition is a bad thing. You cannot be temperate in the use of alcohol if you have none. Nor is sobriety a virtue in you if you lock up the wine-cellar and throw the keys down the well. Very well; then will you do without alcohol or without temperance? There is the choice; and I have made mine.

Besides, we are all for liberty down here, individualists to a man. Give us a loophole to avoid compulsion and we use it. One of the most frequently exercised of my magisterial functions is to certify conscientious objections to the Vaccination Act. I do it against the grain. A doctor told me the other day that he believed smallpox had reached the end of its tether, and was on the ebb. I am sure I hope so, lest there should be one day a bad outbreak among these liberty men. I must have signed away the chances of hundreds of children, who, by the way, are not of an age to consent. I never fail to point out the risk; but the Court awards it and the law allows it; so I sign.

There is much to be said for Anarchy in the abstract, nothing at all in the concrete. Mr. Smillie, however, appears to favour it, raw, rough and ready. In that he is precocious, and, like the rathe primrose, will "forsaken die." He will rend the Labour party in twain from the top to the bottom, and will see the agricultural vote drop off his industrials just as it had begun to adhere to them. I know the peasantry. They will never strike for political ends, for though they are not quick to see the consequences of hypothetical actions, they do see that if you make Parliamentary government impossible you make a Labour majority not worth having.

And another thing: Mr. Smillie and his friends may want a revolution, but Hodge and his most certainly do not. They want to earn their livelihood, pay their way, and dig their plots of ground. No more warfare for them. I dare say I shall be sorry for Mr. Smillie when the time comes; but I may have to be still more sorry for my country first. I can't help hoping, however, when it comes to the point that his feet will be a little colder than his head seems to be just now.

LA PETITE PERSONNE

No letter-writer's stage can at any time be called empty, because upon it you necessarily have at all times two persons at least: the mover of the figures and the audience, the puppeteer and the puppetee, the letter-writer and the letter-reader. The play presented is, therefore, a play within a play: like the *Mousetrap* in *Hamlet*, like *Pyramus and Thisbe* in *A Midsummer Night's Dream*, like the romantic drama of *Gayferos and Melisandra* which Don Quixote witnessed with a select company of acquaintance at an inn. The temperament of this presented spectator, himself or herself a person of the scene, is always reflected in the entertainment when the letter-writer is a sensitive artist. So Horace Walpole's comedy varies according as it goes before Sir Horace Mann in Florence or Lady Upper-Ossory at Ampthill; so, more delicately, does Madame de Sévigné's. There are blacker strokes in the dialogue when Bussy is to see the play; there is always idolatry implied, and sometimes anxiety, if the spoilt child of Provence is the audience. It is this *chère bonne*, this Madame de Grignan, nine times out of ten, who is queen of the entertainment. You have to reckon with her upon her throne of degrees, set up there like Hippolita, Duchess of Athens, to be propitiated and, if possible, diverted. For her sake, not for ours, her incomparable mother beckons from the wings character after character, and gives each his cue, having set the scene with her exquisite art. In a few cases her anxiety to please spoils the effects. As we should say, she "laboured" the Cardinal de Retz. The sour-faced beauty would have none of him. But that is a rare case, one in which predilection betrayed her. Madame de Sévigné had a weakness for the Cardinal. It is very seldom that the lightest hand in the world fails her at a portrait. Her great successes are her thumb-nail sketches: she will be remembered by Picard in the hayfield so long as the world knows how to laugh. One of her best, because one of her tenderest, is the *petite personne*.

The name is Charles de Sévigné's, but his mother takes it up after him, and makes better play with it. Charles writes from Les Rochers in December, 1675—Madame being really ill for once in her life with "a nice little rheumatism," and Charles her amanuensis—"in the room of la Plessis," that striving lady, too, was ill, or thought she was—"we have had lately a very pretty young party (*une petite personne fort jolie*) whose good looks don't at all remind us of that divinity. At her instigation we have started *Reversis*: now, instead of knaves, we talk about jacks." He adds a stroke too good to be lost, though his mother might have left it out. "To give you a notion of her age and quality, she has just confided to us that the day after Easter Eve was a Tuesday. She thought that over, then said, 'No—it was a Monday!' Then, judging by the look of us that that wouldn't do either, 'Heavens, how stupid! Of course—it was a Friday!' That is the kind of party we are. If you wouldn't mind sending us word what day of the week you believe it to have been, you will save us a great deal of discomfort." The stage is the brisker for the coming in of this pretty *soubrette*.

Madame de Sévigné, meantime, is in a discomfort of her own. It takes her some ten days to absorb the *petite personne*, but then she fixes her for ever. Nobody can wish to know more about a young party than this:

> "*Christmas Day* (1675).... I still have that nice child here. She lives on the other side of the park; her mother is the good-wife Marcile's daughter—but you won't remember her. The mother lives at Rennes, but I shall keep her here. She plays *trictrac, reversis*; she is quite pretty, quite innocent, and called Jeannette. She is no more trouble than Fidèle."

Quite pretty, quite innocent and called Jeannette! *Quid Plura?* Need I say who Fidèle was? Fidèle is a shrewd touch of Madame's, put in, as I guess, to placate the hungry-eyed Goddess of Grignan; but it does clinch the portrait. All that one needs to know of the nature, parentage, and upbringing of a *petite personne* is in these two letters.

Immediately upon her entry the comedy begins, with Mademoiselle du Plessis in a leading part. "... La Plessis has a quartan fever. It is pretty to see her jealous fury when she comes here and finds the child with me. The fuss there is to have my stick or muff to hold! But enough of these nothings...."

> It was of nothings that the vexed days of Mlle. du Plessis must exist. An elderly virgin, evidently; stiff, gauche, full of *guinderie*, says Madame, "*et de l'esprit fichu*." Everybody made game of her at Les Rochers. As we shall see, the servants knew that very well. Charles is always witty at her expense. Madame de Grignan once slapped her.

Meanwhile, here's another vignette, a Chardin picture—you will find nothing by Greuze of this *petite personne*. "... What do you think of the handy little lady we were telling you of, who couldn't make out what the day after Easter Eve was? She is a dear little rosebud of a thing who delights us."

"'In six years to come she'll be twenty years old!' I wish you could see her in the mornings, eating a hunk of bread-and-butter as long as from here to Easter, or, after dinner, crunching up two green apples with brown bread...."

But now the clowns come tumbling in, to turn over the poor du Plessis. "... Mlle. du Plessis will die of the *petite personne*. Being more than half dead of jealousy already, she is always at my people to find out how I treat her. Not one of them but has a pin ready. One says that I love her as much as I do you; another that I have her to sleep with me—which would assuredly be a notable sign of affection! They swear that I am taking her to Paris, that I kiss her, am mad about her; that the Abbé is giving her 10,000 *livres*; that if she had but 20,000 *écus* I should marry her to my son. That is the sort of thing; and they carry it so far that we can't help laughing at it. The poor lady is ill with it all."

To the same letter Charles adds his scene in the farce: "La Plessis said to Rahuel (he was the concierge) yesterday that she had been gratified at dinner to find that Madame had turned the child out of her seat and put herself in the place of honour. And Rahuel, in his Breton way: 'Nay, Miss, there's no wonder. 'Tis an honour to your years, naturally. Besides, the little girl is one of the house, as you might say. Madame looks on her almost as she might be Madame de Grignan's little sister.'"

La Plessis, in fact, agonised, and the way was made for the great scene— so good a scene that I think it must have been bagged for the theatre. Labiche must surely have lifted it. It is Charles de Sévigné's masterpiece.

> "The young party here, when she saw how my mother's pains increased towards night, thought that the best thing she could do for her was to cry—which she did. She is that sort, and always the focus of jealousy for la Plessis, who tries to recommend herself to my mother by hating her like the devil. This is what happened yesterday. My mother was dozing quietly in bed; the child, the Abbé and I were by the fire. In came La Plessis. We warned her to come quietly, and she did, and was half across the room when my mother coughed, and then asked for her handkerchief to get rid of some phlegm. The child and I jumped up to get it, but La Plessis was too quick for us, rushed to the bed, and instead of putting the thing to my mother's lips, caught hold of her nose with it, and pinched it so hard that the poor dear cried

out with the pain. She couldn't help being sniffy with the old fuss who had hurt her so—nor laughing at her afterwards. If you had seen this little comedy you would have laughed too."

I should like to know who wouldn't have laughed to tears, after it was over. The scene is priceless.

But all the same, it is not Madame de Sévigné's *genre*. She is mistress of the chuckle, not of the *fou rire*; and La Plessis is not one of her best characters. The *petite personne*, however, is; and I must give a very pretty scene, quite in her own manner, where she is half laughing at the child and half in love with her too.

"The *petite personne* is still here, and always delightful. She has a sharp little wit of her own, too, as new as a young chick's. We enjoy telling her things, for she knows nothing at all, and it makes a kind of game to enlighten her on all sides—with a word or two about the Universe, or about Empires, or countries, or kings, or religions, or wars, or Fate, or the map. There's a pretty jumble of facts to put tidily away in a little head which has never seen a town, nor even a river, and has never really supposed that the world went any farther than the end of the park! But she is delicious. I was telling her to-day about the taking of Wismar; and she understands quite well that we are sorry about it because the King of Sweden is our ally. See how wildly we amuse ourselves."

The last sentence is for the *chère bonne's* benefit, who was very capable herself of being jealous of the *petite personne*. I fancy the touch about Fidèle was put in with the same object. She had to be infinitely careful with the *chère bonne's* black dogs.

In another month the *petite personne* is so far advanced that she can be secretary to her patroness, whose poor hand is too swollen to write. Elaborate perambulations introduce her to the *chère bonne*. "My son has gone to Vitré on some business or other. That is why I give his functions of secretary over to the little lady of whom I have often told you, and who begs you to be pleased to allow her, with great respect, to kiss your hands." That, I should think, was courtesy enough even for the pouting great lady of Provence. In a later letter she kisses Madame de Grignan's *left* hand; so it is written—by herself, but to dictation. Thus the proper distances were kept by one as humane as Madame de Sévigné when she was dealing with her daughter on the other side of idolatry.

But she herself and the child are on better terms than such discipline would imply. In February: "... My letters are so full of myself that it bores me to have them read over. You have too much taste not to be bored too. So I shall stop: even the child is laughing at me now." And then in March: "... My son has left us—we are quite alone, the child and I—reading, writing, and saying our prayers." A jolly little picture of still and gentle life. No Greuze there.

The idyll ends in tears, but not just yet. Two days before she leaves Brittany, having "neither rhyme nor reason in my hands," she makes use of the *petite personne* for the last time: "the most obliging child in the world. I don't know what I should have done without her. She reads me what I like—quite well; she writes as you see; she is fond of me; she is willing; she can talk about Madame de Grignan. In fact, you may love her on my assurance." And then the poor little dear puts in her little word for herself to propitiate this formidable Countess in Provence:

"That would make me very happy, Madame, and I am sure that you must envy my joy to be with your mother. She has been pleased to make me write all that praise of myself, though I was rather ashamed to do it. But I am very unhappy that she is going away."

Madame resumes the pen: "... The child, desired to converse with you ..."—which one may or may not believe. If, as I feel sure, she was bidden to the task, I don't see how she could possibly have brought it off better than in those demure phrases. But is she not a dear little creature?

Then came the dreadful day, the 24th of March, and Madame's coach and six horses carry her to Laval on her way to Paris. She stays there for the night and writes, of course, to her *chère bonne*: "... They carried off the *petite personne* early this morning to save me the outcries of her grief. They were the sobs of a child, so natural that they moved me. I dare say she is dancing about now, but for two days she has been in floods, not having been able to learn restraint from me!" Madame, as we know, had abundantly the gift of tears, and was assuredly none the worse for it.

In Paris, Corbinelli was secretary for a time; but she regretted the *petite personne*. "... I don't like a secretary who is cleverer than I am.... The child suited me much better."

And there the happy little figurine, having danced her hour at Les Rochers, leaves the stage. Other *petites personnes* there are—one the sister of *La Murinette Beauté*, who got on so well with M. de Rohan, and was a lady of Madame de Chaulnes', and presently married a respectable gentleman, a M. de le Bedoyère of Rennes. But these are too high levels for the granddaughter of the good-wife Marcile. That *petite personne*, moreover, was a rather sophisticated young lady. One would never have seen her, in the mornings, munching a hunk of bread-and-butter "as long as from here to Easter." No; Jeannette has fulfilled her part, providing a whiff of marjoram and cottage flowers for the castle chambers. She has read, written and said her prayers. She has the firm outline, the rosy cheeks, the simplicity of a Watteau peasant-girl—nothing of the Greuze languish, with its hint of a *cruche cassée*. She is as fresh as a March wind. Let us believe that she found a true man to relish her prettiness and sharp little wits.

A FOOL OF QUALITY

Tom Coryat, the "single-soled, single-souled and single-shirted observer of Odcombe," having finally bored his neighbours in the country past bearing, was volleyed off upon a tempest of their yawns to London. Exactly when that was I can't find out, but I suppose it to have been in the region of 1605.

In London he set up for a wit, was enrolled in "The Right Worshipful Fraternity of Sireniacal Gentlemen," who met at "The Sign of the Mere-maide in Bread Streete"; had John Donne and Ben Jonson among his convives, and may well have seen Shakespeare and heard him talk, if he did talk. How he appeared himself we can only guess, but I conceive his position in the society to have been that of Polonius in the convocation of politic worms, as one, namely, where he was eaten rather than eating. That, if it was so, may have determined him to make a name for himself by what was his strongest part, namely, his feet.

In 1608 he, the "Odcombian leg-stretcher," did indeed travel "for five months, mostly on foot, from his native place of Odcombe in Somerset, through France, Savoy, Italy, Rhetia, Helvetia, some parts of High Germany, and the Netherlands, making in the whole 1975 miles." He started on the 14th May and was in London again on the 3rd October, and if indeed he did travel mostly on foot, I call it a very creditable performance. The result was a book more talked of than read. "Coryat's Crudities, hastily gobbled up in five months' travels ... newly digested in the hungry aire of Odcombe in his county of Somerset, and now dispersed to the nourishment of the travelling members of this Kingdom." So runs the text of a Palladian title-page, surrounded by emblems of adventure which support a *vera effigies* of Tom himself. He shows there as a beady-eyed bonhomme of thirty-five or so, with a Jacobean beard, and his hair brushed back and worn long, like that of our present-day young men.

The book published, the Sireniacal Gentlemen took off their coats and took up their battledores. Their gibes and quirks are all printed in my edition, and are better reading than the book itself. Coryat was a cockscomb and scorned a straight sentence. A rule of his was: "Never use one adjective if three will do." So far as I know he was the first Englishman who travelled for the fun or the glory of the thing, unless Fynes Moryson anticipated him in those also, as he certainly did in travelling and writing about it. But I think it more probable that Moryson went abroad to improve his mind. I don't think Coryat had any notion of that. Foppery may have moved him, vanity perhaps; in any case there can be no comparison between them. Moryson is thorough, Coryat is not. Moryson is often dull, Coryat seldom. Moryson was a student, Coryat a cockscomb. Moryson was a plain man, Coryat a euphuist of the first water. I haven't the least doubt but that Shakespeare met him at the Mermaid—he called himself a friend of Ben Jonson's—and took the best of him. You will find him in *Love's Labour's Lost* as well as in *All's Well*. For a foretaste of his quality take a small portion of his first sentence, the whole of which fills a page: "I was imbarked at Dover, about tenne of the clocke in the morning, the fourteenth of May 1608, and arrived at Calais ... about five of the clocke in the afternoone, after I had varnished the exterior parts of the ship with the excrementall ebullitions of my tumultuous stomach...." There is more about it, but that will do. Shakespeare can never have missed such a man as that.

Coryat's abiding sensation throughout his travels was astonishment, not at the things which he saw, but rather that he from Odcombe in Somerset should be seeing them. He can never get over it. Here am I, Odcombian Tom, face to face with Amiens Cathedral, with the tombs of the kings at Saint Denis, at Fountaine Beleau cheek by jowl with Henri IV., crossing in a litter the "stupendious" Mont Cenis, pacing the Duomo of Milan, disputing with a Turk in Lyons, with a Jew in Padua, to the detriment of their religions, "swimming" in a gondola on the Grand Canal: here I am, and now what about it? There is always an imported flavour of Odcombe about it. He brings it with him and sprinkles it like scent. He is careful at every stage of his journey to give you the mileage from his own door; his measure of a city's quality is its worth to him as a gift were Odcombe the alternative. Few cities indeed survive the test. Mantua stood a fair chance. "That most sweet Paradise, that *domicilium Venerum et Charitum*," did so ravish his senses and tickle his spirits, he says, that he would desire to live there and spend the remainder of his days "in some divine meditations among the sacred Muses," but for two things, "their grosse idolatry and superstitious ceremonies, which I detest, and the love of Odcombe in Somersetshire, which is so deare unto me that I preferre the very smoak thereof before the fire of all other places under the sunne." So much for Mantua; but Venice, before whose "incomparable and most decantated majestie" his pen faints— Venice beats Odcombe, or something very much like it. He decides that should "foure of the richest mannors of Somersetshire" have been offered him if he would have undertaken not to see Venice, he would have gone without the manors. Odcombe, you see, is not put in question here. He was afraid to risk it.

> When he came home he hung up his pair of shoes in the
> chancel of Odcombe Church, and they may be there to this
> day for all I know.

The Sireniacal Gentlemen made great sport of him.

> If any aske in verse what soar I at?
> My Muse replies The praise of Coryat— —

so John Gyfford begins,

> A work that will eternise thee till God come
> And for thy sake the famous parish Odcombe— —

so George Sydenham ends. Ben Jonson is not represented at the revels, and Inigo Jones lets his high spirits run away with him beyond the bounds of modern printing. Donne is not at his best:

> Lo, here's a man worthy indeed to travell
> Fat Libian plaines, strangest China's gravell;
> For Europe well hath seen him stirre his stumpes,
> Turning his double shoes to simple pumpes.

—the wit of which escapes me. Better is the conceit of

> What had he done, had he e'er hugged th' ocean
> With swimming Drake or famous Magelan,
> And kiss'd that unturn'd cheeke of our old mother,
> Since so our Europe's world he can discover?

The "unturn'd cheeke of our old mother!" The New World should be pleased with that.

In 1615 he made a much further flight, and was to be heard of at "the Court of the most Mighty Monarch, the Great Mogul," whence he wrote to, among other people, the High Seneschal of the "Right Worshipful Fraternity of Sireniacal Gentlemen that meet the first Friday of every month at the Signe of the Mere-maide in Bread-Streete." In this particular letter he greets by name Mr. John Donne, "the author of two most elegant Latine Bookes," Master Benjamin Jonson, the poet, at his chamber in the Blacke Friars, Mr. Samuel Purkas, and Mr. Inigo Jones, and signs himself "the Hierosolymitan—Syrian—Mesopotamian —Armenian—Median—Parthian—Persian—Indian—Leggestretcher of Odcomb in Somerset." The news he gives of "the most famigerated Region of all the East, the ample and large India," is various and occasionally incredible, but none the worse perhaps for that. You must allow the leg-stretcher to be something also of a leg-puller. The Great Mogul had elephant-fights twice a week, we learn. He might well do so if we could believe that he maintained three thousand of them "at an unmeasurable charge." Proceeding, nevertheless, to measure it, Coryat finds it works out at £10,000 a day, which is pretty good even for the Mogul. He also had a thousand wives, "whereof the chiefest (which is his Queene) is called Normal." I like her name. Coryat rode on an elephant, "determining one day (by God's leave) to have my picture expressed in my next book, sitting upon an elephant." But the voyage to the East was one too many for "the ingenious perambulator," and he died of a flux at Surat in December, 1617. Certain English merchants offered him refreshments. "Sack, sack, is there any such thing as sack? I pray you give me some sack." They did; the dysentery was upon him at the time. Even as Sir John might have done did he, and was buried "under a little monument." *Sic exit Coryatus*, says his biographer.

No sooner was he dead than his fellow Sireniacks fell upon his reputation and tore it to shreds.

> He was the imp, whilst he on earth surviv'd,
> From whom this West-World's pastimes were deriv'd;
> He was in city, country, field and court
> The well of dry-trimm'd jests, the pump of sport.

So writes the Water Poet. Another wag trounces his Crudities:

> Tom Coriat, I have seen thy Crudities,
> And methinks very strangely brewed it is,
> With piece and patch together glued it is;
> And now (like thee) ill-favour'd hued it is.
> In many a line I see that lewd it is,
> And therefore fit to be subdued it is—

and much more to the same effect.

Coryat's "natalitial place," as it happens, is very near to mine, and I find something to love in a man who can never forget it. He was a cockscomb, he was an ass; but he preferred the West of England to Italy. He called James I., our king, the "refulgent carbuncle of Christendom," and Prince Charles "the most glittering chrysolite of our English diademe" Both are hard sayings.

SHERIDAN AS MANIAC

All allowances made for the near alliance of great wits—"the lunatic, the lover, and the poet"—there comes a point where the vagaries of temperament overlap and are confounded, and where the historian, at least, must take a line. None of Sheridan's biographers, and he has had, as I think, more than his share, refer to an eclipse of his rational self which he undoubtedly suffered; probably because it was not made public until the other day. Yet there have always been indications of the truth, as when, on his death-bed, he told Lady Bessborough that his eyes would be looking at her through the coffin-lid. Being the woman she was, she probably believed him, or thought that she did. It is from her published letters that we may now understand what reason she had for believing him.

These letters are contained in the correspondence of Lord Granville Leveson-Gower, who was our Ambassador in Paris on and off between 1824 and 1841, a correspondence published in 1916, in two hefty volumes. The period covered is from 1781 to 1821, and the documents are mainly the letters to him of Lady Bessborough, which reveal a relation between the pair so curious that, to me, it is extraordinary that nobody should have called attention to them before. I can only account for that by considering that the letters, which are very long, and the volumes, which are very heavy, do not readily yield what store of sweetness they possess, and that those in particular of Lord Granville Gower have no store of sweetness to yield. They are the wooden letters of a wooden young man. He may have been a beautiful young man, and an estimable young man; but he was insensitive, dull, and a prig. The best things he ever did in his days were to be belettered by Lady Bessborough and married, finally, to her witty and sensible niece.

Meantime, there is no need to disguise the fact, since we have it in cold print, that the acquaintance of the couple, begun at Naples in 1794 as a flirtation, developed rapidly, on the lady's side, into a love affair which was only ended by her death. In 1794, when it all began, Lady Bessborough was thirty-two, had been married for fourteen years, and had four children. Granville Gower was twenty, well born, rich, exceedingly good-looking, and with no excuse for not knowing all about it. In fact, he knew it perfectly, and was not afraid to allude to himself as Antinous. We hear more than enough of his fine blue eyes from Lady Bessborough—and perhaps he did too. She, in her turn, was to hear, poor soul, more than her own heart could bear. All that need be said about that is that, being the woman she was, it was to be expected. And exactly what sort of woman she was she herself puts upon record, in April, 1812, in the following words:—

"*Pour la rareté du fait et la bizarrerie des hommes*, I must
put down what I dare tell nobody—I should be so much
ashamed of it were it not so ridiculous. At this present
April, 1812, in my fifty-first year, I am courted, follow'd,
flatter'd, and made love to *en toutes les formes*, by four
men—two of them reckoned sensible, and one of the two
whom I have known half my life—Lord Holland, Ward,
young M——n, and little M——y. Sir J.C. wanted to marry
me when I was fifteen; so from that time to this—36 years, a
pretty long life—I have heard or spoke that language; and
for 17 years of it lov'd almost to Idolatry the only man from
whom I could have wish'd to hear it, the man who has
probably lov'd me least of all those who have profess'd to
do so—tho' once I thought otherwise."

Arrant sentimentalist, born and trained flirt, as this confession shows her to have been, it also shows that she lived to rue it. She rued more than that, for she was the mother of Lady Caroline Lamb; and if anything more need be said of her misfortunes, let it be added that she was sister to Georgiana of Devonshire. Nevertheless, it is impossible to read her letters with her wooden young lord without seeing that she had a good heart, if a very weak head. She loved much; and for those whom she loved—her sister, her children, Granville Gower—she was ready to dare all things, and fail in most. Of her husband there is nothing to tell, for she hardly names him, except to say that he has the gout. Not much is known of him, and nothing but good. Horace Walpole wrote of his marriage in 1780: "I know nothing to the prejudice of the young lady; but I should not have selected for so gentle and very amiable a man a sister of the empress of fashion, nor a daughter of the Goddess of Wisdom." The goddess of wisdom was her formidable and trenchant mother, Lady Spencer.

But I don't intend to follow the vain stages of her sentimental pilgrimage in pursuit of Lord Granville Gower's heart, vain because apparently the young man had not such an organ at her disposal. It was not, perhaps, for nothing that they exchanged reflections upon *Les Liaisons Dangereuses*. A new Choderlos de Laclos would get a new sentimental novel out of the Granville Gower correspondence; or it may be taken as it stands for a recovered Richardson, quite as long as *Sir Charles Grandison* and much more amusing—for the poor lady is often witty. The affair dragged on, with much scandal, much whispering about it and about, until 1809, when the hero of it married Lady Harriet Cavendish, his mistress's niece. J.W. Ward, one of her lovers, according to her, sharply sums it up in a letter to Mrs. Dugald Stewart: "Lord Granville Leveson is going to marry Lady Harriet Cavendish. Lady Bessborough resigns, I presume, in favour of her niece. I have not heard what are supposed to be the secret articles of the treaty, but it must be a curious document." It was in 1812, as I have said, that she wrote out the pathetic confession of what we must suppose to have been the truth.

But I intended to write about Sheridan. This correspondence reveals him as the evil genius of Lady Bessborough's life; and perhaps, if all the truth were known, she may have been the evil genius of his, or one of them, anyhow. She had adventures with him behind her in 1794, when she began adventures anew; for they became intimate at Devonshire House, where, as the crony of Charles Fox, he was always at hand. The Duchess herself was one of his familiars. His initials for her, in letter-writing, were T.L., which a biographer pleasantly interprets as "True Love." The sisters, Countess and Duchess, shared in all good and evil things, and they seem to have shared Sheridan. His chosen initial for Lady Bessborough's address was "F," her second name being Frances. Mr. Sichel prints a letter from him to her, and guesses it to be of 1788. Extracts will suffice for the judicious: "I must bid 'oo good-night, for by the light passing to and fro near your room I hope you are going to bed and to sleep happily with a hundred little cherubs fanning their white wings over you in approbation of your goodness. Yours is the sweet, untroubled sleep of purity." It is to be feared that she could swallow this over-succulent stuff. A very little more will do for us: "And yet, and yet—Beware! Milton will tell you that even in Paradise serpents found their way to the ear of slumbering innocence. Then, to be sure, poor Eve had no watchful guardian to pace up and down beneath her windows.... And Adam, I suppose—was at Brooks's ... I shall be gone before your hazel eyes are open to-morrow...."

Lady Duncannon, as she was then, lived in Cavendish Square. Sheridan's leaguer of the house is thus betrayed. He never again left either her or it alone for long, but beset them until his death. Bitterly enough she was to rue that dalliance with the vainest sentimentalist ever begotten in Ireland or fostered in England. His wife, as lovely as a Muse and with the voice of a seraph, was to die; he was to adore, pursue, and capture another; but he never let Lady Bessborough go, and the antics of his mortified vanity were to lead her as far into the mire as any woman could go without suffocation. Such experiences may be common enough; it is rare to have them so nakedly portrayed as they are in this lady's letters, and not easy to avoid the conclusion that she made use of them to pique her wooden Antinous into some more active kind of pose than that of allowing himself to be adored.

Sheridan was forty-three and married to his second wife when Lady Bessborough fell in with Antinous at Naples; but it was not until the attachment of those two had become a notoriety that he began to make scenes about it. In 1798, when Granville Gower was in Berlin, Lady Bessborough writes to him that she had been at a concert at Sheridan's. "It was as pleasant as anything of the sort can be to me, as I sat by Fitzpatrick and Grey, who always amuse me. Sheridan says, when he found I did not come to town, he imagined that you had interdicted my coming till your return, and is always asking me whether what I am doing is allowed." That was March 12th; between that and the 17th she seems to have met Sheridan every day and nearly every night. "I must tell you, by the by … that I am in great request this year…. I have had three *violent* declarations of love—one from an old man, another from a very young one, and the third between the other two…. Pray come back. If you stay long in Prussia, Heaven knows what may happen."

In August of the same year she writes again. "Sheridan call'd in the morning and found out that I was alone, and told me he would dine with me. I thought, of course, he was in joke, but, *point du tout*, he arriv'd at dinner, dined, and stayed the whole evening. He was very pleasant, but—it was not you, and the seeing anybody only increas'd my regrets, which I suppose were pretty visible, for every five minutes he kept saying: 'How I am wasting all my efforts to entertain you, while you are grieving that you cannot change me into *Lord Leveson*. You would not be so grim if he was beaming on you.' At length, as I thought he was preparing to pass the night as well as the evening with me, and as he began to make some fine speeches I did not quite approve of, I order'd my Chair, to get rid of him. This did not succeed, for as I had no place to go to, he follow'd me about to Anne's and Lady D——'s, where I knew I should not be let in, and home again. But, luckily, I got in time enough to order every one to be denied, and ran upstairs, while I heard him expostulating with the porter…." It does not appear, from this narrative, that the hunted fair was seriously annoyed at being hunted, and the implication of Lord Granville in the unpleasant business is patent. Next year she has asked her persecutor to help Antinous at his election, for his reply, beginning "Dear Traitress," is given here.

After that, peace or silence, until 1802, when Sheridan changed his tactics.

"The opera was beautiful…. The Prince paid us two visits, but our chief company were Hare, Grey, and Sheridan, the latter persecuting me in every pause of the music and telling me he knew such things of you, could give me such incontrovertible proofs of your falsehood, and not only falsehood but treachery to me, that if I had one grain of pride or spirit left I should fly you. And guess what I answered, you who call me jealous. I told him I had such entire reliance on your faith, such confidence in your truth, that I should doubt my own eyes if they witness'd against your word. He pitied me, and said: 'How are the mighty fallen,' and then went on telling me things without end to drive me mad." That was in March. In August she writes, actually under siege: "Here I am quite alone in C. Square … no carriage to watch for, no rap at the door … and alas! no chance of hearing your step upon the stair…. Whilst I was regretting all this, suddenly, the knock did come, to my utter astonishment. I ran to the stair, and in a moment heard Sheridan's voice. I do not know why, but I took a horror of seeing him, and hurried Sally down to say I was out. I heard him answer: 'Tell her I call'd twice this morning, and want particularly to see her, for I know she is at home.' Sally protested I was out, and S. answered: 'Then I shall walk up and down before the door till she comes in,' and there he is walking sure enough. It is partly all the nonsense he talk'd all this year, and the hating to see any one when I cannot see you, that makes me dislike letting him in so much."

He solemnly did sentry-go for nearly an hour, she goes on to say. In that hour he was in his fifty-first year, she in her fortieth.

If she revealed these sorry doings to Antinous with the view of fanning embers, she did not succeed in drawing more than a languid protest from him. "As to Sheridan, in the morning I purposely staid in my room till the time of our setting out, and only saw him as I was getting into the carriage, so had nothing more to tell…. You say I am not angry enough. I am provok'd, vex'd, and asham'd. To feel more deeply I must care for the person who offends me…." I cannot myself read either vexation or shame in her reports. Provocation I can and do read—but it is not she who is provoked.

In 1804, Antinous in Petersburg, there are new antics to record. "You will think I live at the play; I am just return'd from Drury Lane…. Sheridan persists in coming every night to us. He says one word to my sister; then retires to the further corner of the box, where with arms across, deep and audible sighs, and sometimes *tears*! he remains without uttering and motionless, with his eyes fix'd on me in the most marked and distressing manner, during the whole time we stay. To-night he followed us in before the play begun, and remained as I tell you thro' the play and farce. As we were going I dropped my shawl and muff; he picked them up and with a look of ludicrous humility presented them to Mr. Hill to give me." And this was the author of *The School for Scandal*.

Next year, being that of Trafalgar, and Sheridan's fifty-fourth, he began a course of persecution which definitely marks an access of dementia. The affair took an acute turn suddenly, and I don't intend to say more about it than that it took the form of anonymous and obscene letters, some of them addressed to Lady Bessborough's daughter, Caroline, then a child, some to herself, some to the children of the Duchess of Devonshire. The letters, which continued throughout the year, were signed with the names of friends — a Mr. Hill, J.W. Ward, and others. Some were sent out signed with her name. The editor of the correspondence says that "Lady Bessborough was subsequently convinced by evidence which appeared to her conclusive that Sheridan was the writer." There can be no doubt of that whatever, and as all the detail is in the published correspondence, little more need be said. The wooden Antinous, in Petersburg, for his sole comment, writes as follows: "I learn with sorrow that you are still subjected to vexations from anonymous letters, etc. I suppose that Sheridan is the author, though one would have imagined that, however depraved his morals, and however malignant might be his mind, he would have had *good taste* enough not to have resorted to such a species of vengeance." And that was all the fire to be blown into Antinous. "Good taste" in the circumstances is comic.

By the end of the season of the same year, however, Sheridan seems to have found out what he had done, and Lady Bessborough also sufficient self-respect to have helped him find it out. This is what happened on July 12th, at a ball. "I sat between Prince Adolphus and Mr. Hill at supper; Sheridan sat opposite, looking by turns so supplicating and so fiercely at me that everybody round observ'd it and question'd me about it. I could only say what was so, that he was very drunk. When I got up, he seiz'd my arm as I pass'd him, begging me to shake hands with him. I extricated myself from his grasp and pass'd on; he soon after follow'd and began loudly reproaching me for my *cruelty*, and asking why I would not shake hands. I was extremely distress'd, but at last told him his own sagacity might explain to him why I never would, and that his conduct to-night did not tend to alter my determination. I then hurried out of the room, and by way of completely avoiding him, cross'd a very formal circle of old ladies, and went and seated myself between Lady Euston and Lady Beverly. He had the impudence to follow me, and in face of the whole circle to enter into a loud explanation of his conduct, begging my pardon for all the offences he had ever committed against me, either on this night or in former times, and assuring me that he had never ceased loving, *respecting* and adoring me, and that I was the only person he ever really loved…." "Think," she says, "of the dismay of all the formal ladies." But the formal ladies, no doubt, had every reason to know their Devonshire House set; and if society in 1805 would allow Sheridan to be drunk and stay at a ball, it would prefer him maudlin drunk to drunk and disorderly. One is bound to add, too, that Lady Bessborough was a fool, though that, to be sure, is no excuse for Sheridan proving himself both old blackguard and old fool in one.

Next year the Duchess died, and her sister's active persecution appears to have ceased. But Sheridan by no means let her alone. On the contrary, he had the assurance to send as intercessor no less a person than the Prince Regent. "The Prince sent so repeatedly to me, and has been throughout so kind and feeling that I thought it wrong to persist in refusing to see him, so to-day he came soon after two and stayed till six!… He gave me a very pretty emerald ring, which he begg'd me to wear, *to bind still stronger the tie of Brotherhood which he has always claim'd*. In the midst of all this he brought me a message from Sheridan." This, which she describes as a "well-timed Petition for Forgiveness," she had the prudence to wave aside. She said that she had no wish to injure him, and only asked him to keep out of her way, or, if they happened to meet, to cease to persecute her. And that was very well, or would have been so, if she had had any character at all, a quality which she unfortunately had not. In 1807, the following year, she goes out to spend the evening with her daughter, Lady Caroline, now married to William Lamb. "The entrance is, you know, very dark; to my dismay, I saw a ruffian-like looking man following me into the house. I hasten'd upstairs, but to my great dismay he also ascended and enter'd the room immediately after me. It was so dark I could not at first make out who he was. When I did, I was not the better pleas'd with his establishing himself and passing the whole evening with us; but much as I was displeased with him, I was still more so with myself for being unable to resist laughing and appearing entertained (he was so uncommonly clever), tho' I persevered in my determination of not speaking to him. I do not like his having got the entrée there, and think him, even old as he is, a dangerous acquaintance for Caroline. Of course you perceive it was Sheridan." Considering that she suspected him of having written and sent grossly indecent letters to that girl of hers, one would have said that he was even more than a dangerous acquaintance. Light-mindedness here spills over into something rather worse. However, there he was, established, and it was no way to dispossess him to laugh at his jokes.

I must now invite the reader to a farce, and, if he can forget that Sheridan was a grandfather and fifty-six, a very good farce it is. It is 1807, the 28th July. Lady Bessborough is staying with her daughter for her first confinement, and receives a message from Mrs. Sheridan, a rather wild young woman in her way, known to all Devonshire House as Hecca. She goes at midnight,

> "… and was carried up to her bedroom, where we had not sat long when a violent burst at the door announc'd the arrival of Sheridan, not perfectly sober. The most ridiculous scene ensued—that is, ridiculous it would have been if I had not felt myself too indignant and disgusted to be entertain'd. He began by asking my pardon, entreating my mercy and compassion, saying that he was a wretch, and was even at that moment more in love with *me* than with any woman he had ever met with, on which Hecca exclaimed: 'Not excepting me? Why, you always tell me that I am the only woman you were ever in love with.' 'So you are, to be sure, my dear Hecca; you know *that*, of course—you *know* that I love you better than anything on earth.' '*Except* her!' 'Pish, pish, child! Do not talk nonsense.' Then he began again at me, upbraiding me for my cruelty, both for quarrelling with him and setting Hecca against him. The first, I said, I did in my own defence, the other was false, Hecca every now and then coming in with: 'Why, S——, I thought Lady B—— pursued you, and that you reviled all her violence like a second Joseph? So you us'd to tell me.' I cannot give you all the conversation, for it lasted till near three in the morning…. Getting away was the difficulty; he wanted to come down with me, and seiz'd my arm with such violence once before Hecca, that I was obliged to call her maid to help me, and at last only escaped by locking him in."

This sort of thing happened once more, in the same year, at Brocket. On this occasion Sheridan pursued his victim into the nursery, and threw himself on his knees. It gave Lady Bessborough an opportunity which even she could not fail to perceive—and she used it. "I interrupted the most animated professions by showing him the child and asking him if his grandchildren were as pretty as mine. He jump'd up, but with such fury in his looks that I was really frighten'd…" And that may very well be the end: *solvuntur tabulæ risu*. Lord Granville Gower married in 1809, and the confidential correspondence died the death; but Sheridan lingered until 1816, and actually carried on his desperate pursuit within three days of the end. She visited him, and described what took place to Lord Broughton. He assured her, she said, that he should visit her after his death. She asked, "Why, having persecuted her all her life, would he now carry it into death?' 'Because I am resolved you shall remember me.'"[A] The story of his telling her that his eyes would see her through the coffin-lid is well known, and may be apocryphal; but the melodrama is Sheridan all over.

> [Footnote A: Mr. Sichel, in his monumental book on Sheridan, doubts the lady's memory, one of his grounds of doubt being that Sheridan "would not have been likely to have thus behaved before his wife." But Mr. Sichel did not then know what Sheridan was capable of doing before his wife.]

Curiosity rather than edification is served by the publication of such frank revelations as Lady Bessborough's, but that is a matter for her descendants, and was probably considered. What relates to Sheridan is quite another thing. On his death Byron hailed him with eloquent if extravagant praise; he was buried in Westminster Abbey; three long biographies have been written round him, not one of which has failed to do justice to his abilities, and not one pointed out the extent of his moral aberration. Mr. Sichel, the latest of them, says that "he had pursued his own path and spurned the little arts of those who twitted him with roguery." But if the Granville Gower correspondence is to be believed—and how can it not—he was either a very bad rogue or a madman. Sheridan, after all's said, made a great figure in his day, and must stand the racket of it, so to speak. Gossip about Harriet may be left to the idle; but Sheridan belongs to History.

A FOOTNOTE TO COLERIDGE

Coleridge is one of our great men who require many footnotes, for there are characteristics of his which need all the extenuation they can get. How comes it, for instance, that he could write, and not only write but publish, in the same decade, and sometimes in the same year, poetry which is of our very best, and some which for frozen inanity it would be hard to equal anywhere? How could a thinker of his power of brain cover leagues of letter-paper with windy nonsense and mawkish insincerity? And finally, of what quality was the talk of one whose social life was entirely monologue? To the first of these questions Wordsworth perhaps helps with an analogy, but not very far; for it is certain that Wordsworth's opinion of the importance of his own verses was inflexible, whereas Coleridge, having another medium of expression, was by no means so insistent upon publishing. Upon the second, it may be observed that when a philosopher is at the same time a poet, and therefore his own rhapsodist, it is probable that he will charm the understanding of many, but certain that he will bewitch his own. The certainty is clinched when the rhapsodist is without the humorous sense. It was the possession of that which enabled Charles Lamb, who loved him, to see him "Archangel, a little damaged," and even in one dreadful moment of his life to reprove him for a too oleaginous sympathy. Lamb, in fact, was always able to view his friend with clear eyes. In a letter to Manning, enclosing "all Coleridge's letters" to himself, he says that in them Manning will find "a good deal of amusement, to see genuine talent struggling against a pompous display of it." No criticism could be sounder. But Coleridge never wavered from the belief that he was in no phase of his being an ordinary man. If his thoughts were not ordinary thoughts, his imaginings not ordinary imaginings, then his stomach-aches were not ordinary stomach-aches, but strokes of calamity so grievous as to demand from him copious commentary and appeals for more sympathy than is ordinarily given to ordinary men. And, strange to say, he received it. There was that in the "noticeable man with large grey eyes" which drew the love of his friends and the regard of acquaintance. His talk had the quality of his Ancient Mariner's; one could not choose but hear. The accounts which we have of that, however, are mainly sympathetic; it is not so certain how it affected hearers who were not predisposed.

Lately a book has been published, or rather republished, which illustrates Coleridge's relations with a world outside his own. *A House of Letters* (Jarrolds—N.D.), containing a selection of the memoirs and correspondence of Miss Mary Matilda Betham, includes a good many letters from Coleridge, and some few from Charles Lamb which have not so far been recorded elsewhere. Miss Betham, who was born in 1776, was a miniature painter by profession, and so far as can be judged by reproductions a good one. She was a poetess, too, and the compiler of a Biographical Dictionary of Celebrated Women. In 1797 she published a volume of *Elegies*, which in 1802 was sent to Coleridge by his friend Lady Boughton, and of which a short piece, "On a Cloud," transported him. He addressed immediately a blank-verse exhortation "To Matilda Betham, from a Stranger," dated it Keswick, September 9th, 1802, signed it "S.T.C.," and sent it off.

> Matilda! I have heard a sweet tune play'd
> On a sweet instrument—thy Poesie,

it began; and went on to hope—

> That our own Britain, our dear mother Isle,
> May boast one Maid, a poetess indeed,
> Great as th' impassioned Lesbian, in sweet song,
> And O! of holier mind, and happier fate.

That was what he called twining her vernal wreath around the brows of patriot Hope. He concluded with some cautionary lines whose epithets are irresistibly comic:

> Be bold, meek Woman! but be wisely bold!
> Fly, ostrich-like, firm land beneath thy feet.

And for her ultimate reward—

> What nobler meed, Matilda! canst thou win
> Than tears of gladness in a Boughton's eyes,
> And exultation even in strangers' hearts?

> It is a wonderful thing indeed that, having composed *The Ancient Mariner* (1797), *Love* (1799), *Christabel* (1797-1800), and *Kubla Khan* (1798), he should slip back into this eighteenth-century flatulence—but Coleridge could do such things and not turn a hair.

Nevertheless, to a young poetess, a bad poem is still a poem, and means a reader. An acquaintance invited in such terms will thrive, and that of Miss Betham and the Stranger ripened into a friendship. She went to stay at Greta Hall, painted portraits of Mrs. Coleridge and Sara, and of some of the Southeys too. Through them she became acquainted with the Lambs, and if never one of their inner circle, was a familiar correspondent, and had relations with George Dyer, the Morgans, the Thelwalls, Montagues, Holcrofts and others. Altogether Lady Boughton's bow at a venture brought down a goodly quarry for Miss Betham, but many waters were to flow under the restless philosopher before he could swim into her ken again.

It was in 1808, in fact, when he was living in London (at the *Courier* office, 348, Strand), and in the midst of his second course of lectures, that the intercourse was renewed—or rather it is there that *A House of Letters* enables us to pick it up. We find him then writing in this kind of strain to Matilda:—

> "What joy would it not be to you, or to me, Miss Betham, to meet a Milton in a future state, and with that reverence due to a superior, pour forth our deep thanks for the noble feelings he had aroused in us, for the impossibility of many mean and vulgar feelings and objects which his writings had secured us!"

The Americans call that sort of thing poppycock, which seems a useful phrase. No doubt there was more of it, though it is precisely there, without subscription or signature, that the Editor of *A House of Letters* thinks fit to conclude. He has much to learn of the duties of editorship, among other things, as we shall have to note before long, reasonable care in recording and printing his originals. Upon that letter, at any rate, *post* if not *propter*, Miss Betham proposed to the philosopher that he should sit to her, and that, with some demur, he promised to do. An appointment was made to that end, and punctually broken. Then came this letter of excuse, which should have been worth many a miniature, being indeed a full-length portrait done by a master-hand:—

> "Dear Miss Betham,—Not my will, but accident and necessity made me a truant from my promise. I was to have left Merton, in Surrey, at half-past eight on Tuesday morning with a Mr. Hall, who would have driven me in his chaise to town by ten; but having walked an unusual distance on the Monday, and talked and exerted myself in spirits that have been long unknown to me, on my return to my friend's house, being thirsty, I drank at least a quart of lemonade; the consequence was that all Tuesday morning, till indeed two o'clock in the afternoon, I was in exceeding pain, and incapable of quitting my room, or dismissing the hot flannels applied to my body...."

This was no ordinary philosopher; but the chapter is not yet full.

He left Merton, he says, at five, walked stoutly on, was detained an hour and a half on Clapham Common, "in an act of mere humanity," and finally reached Vauxhall.

> "At Vauxhall I took a boat for Somerset House: two mere children were my Charons; however, though against tide, we sailed safely to the landing-place, when, as I was getting out, one of the little ones (God Bless him!) moved the boat. On turning halfway round to reprove him, he moved it again, and I fell back on the landing-place. By my exertions I should have saved myself but for a large stone which I struck against just under my crown and unfortunately in the very same place which had been contused at Melton (*sic*) when I fell backward after learning suddenly and most abruptly of Captain Wordsworth's fate in the *Abergavenny*, a most dear friend of mine. Since that time any great agitation has occasioned a feeling of, as it were, a *shuttle* moving from that part of the back of my head horizontally to my forehead, with some pain but more confusion."

The unction of that blessing called down upon his persecutor is truly Coleridgian. "Melton" is the Editor's rendering of Malta, where Coleridge was when he heard of John Wordsworth's drowning in 1805. He had then kept his bed for a fortnight, or so he told Mrs. Coleridge.

Apparently no meeting took place, as yet another letter, dated 7th May, relates how instead of going to New Cavendish Street, where Miss Betham lived, he went to Old Cavendish Street, where she did not. "I knocked at every door in Old Cavendish Street, not unrecompensed for the present pain by the remembrances of the different characters of voice and countenance with which my question was answered in all gradations, from gentle and hospitable kindness to downright brutality." Further promises and assurances are given, and in July, as we learn from a letter of Southey's, the good Matilda was still high in hopes that her sitter would eventually sit. Her hopes could not have come from Southey, who had none. "You would have found him the most wonderful man living in conversation, but the most impracticable one for a painter, and had you begun the picture it is ten thousand to one that you must have finished it from memory." He was right. When his lectures were over, in June, Coleridge went to Bury St. Edmunds, and by the 9th September he was in Cumberland. "Coleridge has arrived at last, about half as big as the house," Southey writes to his brother on that day. There he cogitated and there began *The Friend*, and there the separation from his wife was finally made.

After the separation, very characteristically, he was less separated from Mrs. Coleridge than he had been for many years. In 1810 he was still in the Lakes, in the summer of which year his wife gives news of him to the poetess. "Coleridge has been with me for some time past, in good health, spirits and humour, but the *Friend* for some unaccountable reason, or for no reason at all, is utterly silent. This, you will easily believe, is matter of perpetual grief to me, but I am obliged to be silent on the subject, although ever uppermost in my thoughts, but I am obliged to bear about a cheerful countenance, knowing as I do by sad experience that to expostulate, or even to hazard one anxious look, would soon drive him hence." Then comes a sidelight on the Wordsworths. "Coleridge sends you his best thanks for the elegant little book; I shall not, however, let it be carried over to Grasmere, for *there* it would soon be *soiled*, for the Wordsworths are woeful destroyers of good books, as our poor library will witness."

But all this was too good to last, and as everybody knows, it did not. In October Coleridge left the Lakes with the Montagues, and almost immediately after that the rupture with the Wordsworths occurred, which involved also the family at Keswick. Southey's letter to Miss Betham giving her an account of the affair has been published by Mr. Dykes Campbell, and is misplaced in *A House of Letters*. The unfortunate philosopher set up his rest with the Morgans, friends of the Lambs, at Hammersmith; and there he was in February, 1811, when Miss Betham conceived her project of getting him as a lion at the party of her friend Lady Jerningham.

Lady Jerningham, blue mother of a bluer daughter (Lady Bedingfield) and sister-in-law of the "Charming Man" of Walpole's and the Misses Berry's acquaintance, was a friend of Miss Betham's of old standing. Several letters of hers are in *A House of Letters*, but many more of her daughter's. Whether it was her ladyship's or Miss Betham's proposal there's no telling now; but Miss Betham, at any rate, did not feel equal to the job, and called in Charles and Mary Lamb to help her. Mary, in the first instance, sounded the philosopher, and with success. I quote from Mr. Lucas's edition of the Lamb letters, as the editor of Miss Betham's misreads and misprints his original. "Coleridge," she writes, "has given me a very cheerful promise that he will wait on Lady Jerningham any day you will be pleased to appoint. He offered to write to you, but I found it was to be done *to-morrow*, and as I am pretty well acquainted with his to-morrows, I thought good to let you know his determination to-day. He is in town to-day, but as he is often going to Hammersmith for a night or two, you had better perhaps send the invitation through me, and I will manage it for you as well as I can. You had better let him have four or five days' previous notice, and you had better send the invitation as soon as you can; for he seems tolerably well just now. I mention all these betters, because I wish to do the best I can for you, perceiving, as I do, it is a thing you have set your heart on."

Charles was next brought in. Mr. Lucas gives his letter (I. 429) to John Morgan, which says, "There—don't read any further, because the letter is not intended for you, but for Coleridge, who might perhaps not have opened it directed to him *suo nomine*. It is to invite C., to Lady Jerningham's on Sunday."

Finally, Coleridge went to the party, and apparently in company, though it is not clear in whose company. This is what Lady Jerningham thought about it:—

> "My dear Miss Betham,—I have been pleased with your friends, tho' (which is not singular) they sometimes fly higher than my imagination can follow. I think the author ought to mix more, I will not say with Fools, but with People of Common Comprehension. His own intellect would be as bright, and what emanated from it more clear. This is perhaps a very impertinent Remark for me to venture at making, but your indulgence invited sincerity."

That letter, I think, whose capitals are particularly graphic, throws the whole party up in a dry light. One can see the rhapsodist talking interminably, involving himself ever deeplier in a web of his own spinning; the great lady gazing in wonder. It is one of the very few impartial witnesses we have to his conversational feats. Nearly all the evidence is tainted either by predisposition in his favour or the reverse. Hazlitt, a mainly hostile witness, says that he talked well on every subject; Godwin on none. One suspects antithesis there. He reports Holcroft as saying that "he thought Mr. C. a very clever man, with a great command of language, but that he feared he did not always affix very precise ideas to the words he used!" Then we have Byron, who wrote for effect, and whose aim was scorn. "Coleridge is lecturing. 'Many an old fool,' said Hannibal to some such lecturer, 'but such as this, never.'" Tom Moore, who met Coleridge at Monkhouse's famous poets' dinner-party, goes no further than to allow that "Coleridge told some tolerable things:" but what Tom wanted was anecdote. Directly Coleridge began upon theory Moore was bored. He shuts him down with a "This is absurd." Rogers was present at that party, but we don't know what he thought about it. He admits that Coleridge was a marvellous talker, however. "One morning when Hookham Frere also breakfasted with me, Coleridge talked for three hours without intermission about poetry, and so admirably that I wish every word he uttered had been written down." But it was not always so well. He says elsewhere that he and Wordsworth once called upon him. Coleridge "talked uninterruptedly for about two hours, during which Wordsworth listened with profound attention, every now and then nodding his head. On quitting the lodging, I said to Wordsworth, 'Well, for my own part, I could not make head or tail of Coleridge's oration; pray, did you understand it?' 'Not one syllable of it,' was Wordsworth's reply."

Keats' account is capital. He met the Sage between Highgate and Hampstead, he says, and "walked with him, at his alderman-after-dinner pace, for near two miles, I suppose. In those two miles he broached a thousand things. Let me see if I can give you a list—nightingales—poetry—on poetical sensation—metaphysics—different genera and species of dreams—nightmare—a dream accompanied with a sense of touch—single and double touch—a dream related—first and second consciousness—the difference explained between will and volition—so say *metaphysicians* from a *want of smoking the second consciousness*—monsters—the Kraken—mermaids—Southey believes in them—Southey's belief too much diluted—a ghost story—Good morning—I heard his voice as he came towards me—I heard it as he moved away—I had heard it all the interval—if it may be called so."

Charles Lamb's is even better. On his way to the city he met Coleridge, and "in spite of my assuring him that time was precious, he drew me within the door of an unoccupied garden by the roadside, and there, sheltered from observation by a hedge of evergreens, he took me by the button of my coat, and closing his eyes, commenced an eloquent discourse, waving his right hand gently, as the musical words flowed in an unbroken stream from his lips. I listened entranced; but the striking of a church-clock recalled me to a sense of duty." Charles cut himself free with a pen-knife, he says, and went off to his office. "Five hours afterwards, in passing the garden on my way home, I heard Coleridge's voice, and on looking in, there he was, with closed eyes—the button in his fingers—his right hand gracefully waving." A good story, at least. This was no company for Lady Jerningham, who demanded clarity, and probably had a good deal to do.

Lastly, we have Coleridge's own confession to Miss Betham that "Bacchus ever sleek and young," as at this time Lamb called him, "pouring down," he went on to say, "goblet after goblet," must have outdone his usual outdoings. Here is the best he can say for himself:—

> "True history will be my sufficient apology. After my return from Lady J.'s on Monday night, or rather morning, I awoke from my short sleep unusually indisposed, and was at last forced to call up the good daughter of the house at an early hour to get me hot water and procure me medicine. I could

not leave my bed till past six Monday evening, when I crawled out in order to see Charles Lamb, and to afford him such poor comfort as my society might perhaps do in the present dejection of his spirits and loneliness."

There is much more to the same effect; and surely it is not often that a philosopher, or even a poet, will treat his post-prandial dumps (to call them so) as a stroke of adverse fortune. Coleridge takes it as an act of God. "This, my dear Miss Betham, waiving all connexion of sentences, is the history of my breach of engagement, of its cause, and of the occasion of that cause." There is much of Mr. Micawber here.

And here, so far as *A House of Letters* can help us, Coleridge's correspondence with Matilda Betham ends. It may well have been the end indeed. From that date onwards the wreck of the thinker and poet slid swiftly down the slope appointed, until he came up, after many bumps, in the hospitable Highgate backwater where he was to end his days. It was a wonderful London which within the same twenty years could harbour three men, like Blake, Coleridge and Shelley, in whom the incondite spirit which we call genius dwelt so near the surface of conscious being, and had such freedom to range. With Blake and Shelley, however, once over the threshold, it was untrammelled—and with Blake at least entirely innocuous to society, except to one drunken soldier who richly deserved what he got. But with Coleridge, throughout his career, one sees it struggling like a fly glued in treacle, pausing often to cleanse its wings. The fly, you adjudge, walked into the treacle. But Coleridge always thought that it was the treacle which had walked over him.

THE CRYSTAL VASE

I have often wished that I could write a novel in which, as mostly in life, thank goodness, nothing happens. Jane Austen, it has been objected, forestalled me there, and it is true that she very nearly did—but not quite. It was a point for her art to make that the novel should have form. Form involved plot, plot a logic of events; events—well, that means that there were collisions. They may have been mild shocks, but persons did knock their heads together, and there were stars to be seen by somebody. In life, in a majority of cases, there are no stars, yet life does not on that account cease to be interesting; and even if stars should happen to be struck out, it is not the collision, nor the stars either, which interest us most. No, it is our state of soul, our mental process under the stress which we care about, and as mental process is always going on, and the state of the soul is never the same for two moments together, there is ample material for a novel of extreme interest, which need never finish, which might indeed be as perennial as a daily newspaper or the *Annual Register*. Why is it, do you suppose, that anybody, if he can, will read anybody else's letter? It is because every man-Jack of us lives in a cage, cut off from every other man-Jack; because we are incapable of knowing what is going on in the mind of our nearest and dearest, and because we burn for the assurance we may get by evidence of homogeneity procurable from any human source. Man is a creature of social instinct condemned by his nature to be solitary. Creatures in all outward respects similar to himself are awhirl about him. They cannot help him, nor he them; he cannot even be sure, for all he may assume it, that they share his hope and calling.

> Ensphered in flesh we live and die,
> And see a myriad souls adrift,
> Our likes, and send our voiceless cry
> Shuddering across the void: "The truth!
> Succour! The truth!" None can reply.

That is the state of our case. We can cope with mere events, comedy, tragedy, farce. The things that happen to us are not our life. They are imposed upon life, they come and go. But life is a secret process. We only see the accretions.

The novel which I dreamed of writing has recently been done, or rather begun, by Miss Dorothy Richardson. She betters the example of Jane Austen by telling us much more about what seems to be infinitely less, but is not so in reality. She dips into the well whereof Miss Austen skims the surface. She has essayed to report the mental process of a young woman's lifetime from moment to moment. In the course of four, if not five, volumes nothing has happened yet but the death of a mother and the marriage of a sister or so. She may write forty, and I shall be ready for the forty-first. Mental process, the states of the soul, emotional reaction—these as they are moved in us by other people are Miss Richardson's subject-matter, and according as these are handled is the interest we can devote to her novels. These fleeting things are Miss Richardson's game, and they are the things which interest us most in ourselves, and the things which we desire to know most about in our neighbours.

But, of course, it won't do. Miss Richardson does not, and cannot, tell us all. A novel is a piece of art which does not so much report life as transmute it. She takes up what she needs for her purpose, and that may not be our purpose. And so it is with poetry—we don't go to that for the facts, but for the essence of fact. The poet who told us all about himself at some particular pass would write a bad poem, for it is his affair to transfigure rather than transmute, to move us by beauty at least as much as by truth. What we look for so wistfully in each other is the raw material of poetry. We can make the finished article for ourselves, given enough matter; and indeed the poetry which is imagined in contemplation is apt to be much finer than that which has passed through the claws of prosody and syntax. The fact, to be short with it, is that literature has an eye upon the consumer. Whether it is marketable or not, it is intended for the public. Now no man will undress in public with design. It may be a pity, but so it is. Undesignedly, I don't say. It would be possible, I think, by analysis, to track the successive waves of mental process in *In Memoriam*. Again, *The Angel in the House* brought Patmore as near to self-explication as a poet can go. Shakespeare's Sonnets offer a more doubtful field of experiment.

What then? Shall we go to the letter-writers—to Madame de Sevigne, to Gray, to Walpole and Cowper, Byron and Lamb? A letter-writer implies a letter-reader, and just that inadequacy of spoken communication will smother up our written words. Madame de Sévigné must placate her high-sniffing daughter, Gray must please himself; Walpole must at any cost be lively, Cowper must be urbane to Lady Hesketh or deprecate the judgment of the Reverend Mr. Newton. Byron was always before the looking-glass as he wrote; and as for Charles Lamb, do not suppose that he did anything but hide in his clouds of ink. Sir Sidney Colvin thinks that Keats revealed himself in his letters, but I cannot agree with him. Keats is one of the best letter-writers we have; he can be merry, fanciful, witty, thoughtful, even profound. He has a sardonic turn of language hardly to be equalled outside Shakespeare. "Were it in my device, I would reject a Petrarchal coronation—on account of my dying day, and because women have cancers?" Where will you match that but from Hamlet? But Keats knew himself. "It is a wretched thing to confess, but it is a very fact, that not one word I can utter can be taken for granted as an opinion growing out of my identical Nature." So I find him in his letters, swayed rather by his fancies than his states of soul, until indeed that soul of his was wrung by agony of mind and disease of body. Revelation, then, like gouts of blood, did issue, but of that I do not now write. No man is sane at such a crisis.

Parva componere magnis, there is a letter contained in *The Early Diary of Frances Burney*(ed. Mrs. A.R. Ellis, 1889), more completely apocalyptic than anything else of the kind accessible to me. Its writer was Maria Allen, daughter of Dr. Burney's second wife, therefore half-sister to the charming Burney girls. She was a young lady who could let herself go, in act as well as on paper, and withal, as Fanny judged her, "flighty, ridiculous, uncommon, lively, comical, entertaining, frank, and undisguised"—or because of it—she did contrive to unfold her panting and abounding young self more thoroughly than the many times more expert. You have her here in the pangs of a love-affair, of how long standing I don't know, but now evidently in a bad state of miss-fire. It was to end in elopement, post-chaise, clandestine marriage, in right eighteenth-century. Here it is in an earlier state, all mortification, pouting and hunching of the shoulder. I reproduce it with Maria's punctuation, which shows it to have proceeded, as no doubt she did herself, in gasps:

> "I was at the Assembly, forced to go entirely against my own Inclination. But I always have sacrificed my own Inclinations to the will of other people—could not resist the pressing Importunity of—Bet Dickens—to go—tho' it proved Horribly stupid. I drank tea at the—told old Turner—I was determined not to dance—he would not

believe me—a wager ensued—half a crown provided I followed my own Inclinations—agreed—Mr. Audley asked me. I refused—sat still—yet followed my own Inclinations. But four couple began—Martin (c'était Lui) was there—yet stupid—n'importe—quite Indifferent—on both sides—Who had I—to converse with the whole Evening—not a female friend—none there—not an acquaintance—All Dancing—who then—I've forgot—n'importe—I broke my earring—how—heaven knows—foolishly enough—one can't always keep on the Mask of Wisdom—well n'importe I danced a Minuet a quatre the latter end of the Eve—with a stupid Wretch—need I name him—They danced cotillions almost the whole Night—two sets—yet I did not join them—Miss Jenny Hawkins danced—with who—can't you guess—well—n'importe———"

There is more, but my pen is out of breath. Nobody but Mr. Jingle ever wrote like that; and in so far as Maria Allen may be said to have had a soul, there in its little spasms is the soul of Maria Allen, with all the *malentendus* of the ballroom and all the surgings of a love-affair at cross-purposes thrown in.

As for Fanny Burney's early diary, its careful and admirable editor claims that you have in it "the only published, perhaps the only existing record of the life of an English girl, written of herself in the eighteenth century." I believe that to be true. It is a record, and a faithful and very charming record of the externals of such a life. As such it is, to me, at least, a valuable thing. If it does not unfold the amiable, brisk, and happy Fanny herself, there are two simple reasons why it could not. First, she was writing her journal for the entertainment of old Mr. Crisp of Chessington, the "Daddy Crisp" of her best pages; secondly, it is not at all likely that she knew of anything to unfold. Nor, for that matter, was Fanny herself of the kind that can unfold to another person. Yet there is a charm all over the book, which some may place here, some there, but which all will confess. For me it is not so much that Fanny herself is a charming girl, and a girl of shrewd observation, of a pointed pen, and an admirable gift of mimicry. She has all that, and more—she has a good heart. Her sister Susan is as good as she, and there are many of Susan's letters. But the real charm of the book, I think, is in the series of faithful pictures it contains of the everyday round of an everyday family. Dutch pictures all—passers-by, a knock at the front door, callers—Mr. Young, "in light blue embroidered with silver, a bag and sword, and walking in the rain"; a jaunt to Greenwich, a concert at home—the Agujari in one of her humours; a masquerade—a very private one, at the house of Mr. Laluze.... Hetty had for three months thought of nothing else ... she went as a Savoyard with a hurdy-gurdy fastened round her waist. Nothing could look more simple, innocent and pretty. "My dress was a close pink Persian vest covered with a gauze in loose pleats...." What else? Oh, a visit to Teignmouth—Maria Allen now Mrs. Ruston; another to Worcester; quiet days at King's Lynn, where "I have just finished *Henry and Frances* ... the greatest part of the last volume is wrote by Henry, and on the gravest of grave subjects, and that which is most dreadful to our thoughts, Eternal Misery...." Terrific novel: but need I go on? There may be some to whom a description of the nothings of our life will be as flat as the nothings themselves—but I am not of that party. The things themselves interest me, and I confess the charm. It is the charm of innocence and freshness, a morning dew upon the words.

The Burneys, however, can do no more for us than shed that auroral dew. They cannot reassure us of our normal humanity, since they needed reassurance themselves.

Where, then, shall we turn? So far as I am aware, to two only, except for two others whom I leave out of account. Rousseau is one, for it is long since I read him, but my recollection is that the *Confessions* is a kind of novel, pre-meditated, selective, done with great art. Marie Bashkirtseff is another. I have not read her at all. Of the two who remain I leave Pepys also out of account, because, though it may be good for us to read Pepys, it is better to have read him and be through with it. There, under the grace of God, go a many besides Pepys, and among them every boy who has ever befouled a wall with a stump of pencil. We are left then with one whom it is ill to name in the same fill of the inkpot, "Wordsworth's exquisite sister," as Keats, who saw her once, at once knew her to be.

In Dorothy Wordsworth's journals, you may have the delight of daily *intercourse—famigliarmente discorrendo*—with one of the purest and noblest souls ever housed in flesh; to that you may add the reassurance to be got from word and implication beyond doubt. She tells us much, but implies more. We may see deeply into ourselves, but she sees deeply into a deeper self than most of us can discern. It is not only that, knowing her, we are grounded in the rudiments of honour and lovely living; it is to learn that human life can be so lived, and to conclude that of that at least is the Kingdom of Heaven.

These journals are for fragments only of the years which they cover, and as such exist for Jan.-May, 1798 (Alfoxden); May-Dec, 1800, Oct.-Dec, 1801, Jan.-July, 1802: all these at Grasmere. They have been printed by Professor Knight, and I have the assurance of Mr. Gordon Wordsworth that what little has been omitted is unimportant. Nothing is unimportant to me, and I wish the whole had been given us; but what we have is enough whereby to trace the development of her extraordinary mind and of her power of self-expression. The latter, undoubtedly, grew out of emotion, which gradually culminated until the day of William Wordsworth's marriage. There it broke, and with it, as if by a determination of the will, there the revelation ceased. A new life began with the coming of Mary Wordsworth to Dove Cottage, a life of which Dorothy records the surface only.

The Alfoxden fragment (20 Jan.-22 May, 1798), written when she was twenty-seven, is chiefly notable for its power of interpreting landscape. That was a power which Wordsworth himself possessed in a high degree. There can be no doubt, I think, that they egged each other on, but I myself should find it hard to say which was egger-on and which the egged. This is the first sentence of it:

> "20 Jan.—The green paths down the hillsides are channels for streams. The young wheat is streaked by silver lines of water running between the ridges, the sheep are gathered together on the slopes. After the wet dark days, the country seems more populous. It peoples itself in the sunbeams."

Here is one of a few days later:

> "23rd.—Bright sunshine; went out at 3 o'cl. The sea perfectly calm blue, streaked with deeper colour by the clouds, and tongues or points of sand; on our return of a gloomy red. The sun gone down. The crescent moon, Jupiter and Venus. The sound of the sea distinctly heard on the tops of the hills, which we could never hear in summer. We attribute this partly to the bareness of the trees, but chiefly to the absence of the singing birds, the hum of insects, that noiseless noise which lives in the summer air. The villages marked out by beautiful beds of smoke. The turf fading into the mountain road."

She handles words, phrases, like notes or chords of music, and never gets her landscape by direct description. One more picture and I must leave it:

"26.— ... Walked to the top of a high hill to see a fortification. Again sat down to feed upon the prospect; a magnificent scene, *curiously* spread out for even minute inspection though so extensive that the mind is afraid to calculate its bounds...."

Coleridge was with them most days, or they with him. Here is a curious point to note. Dorothy records:

"March 7th.—William and I drank tea at Coleridge's. Observed nothing particularly interesting.... One only leaf upon the top of a tree—the sole remaining leaf—danced round and round like a rag blown by the wind."

And Coleridge has in *Christabel*:

The one red leaf, the last of its clan,
That dances as often as dance it can,
Hanging so light, and hanging so high,
On the topmost twig that looks up at the sky.

William, Dorothy, and Coleridge went to Hamburg at the end of that year, but in 1800 the brother and sister were in Grasmere; and the journal which opens with May 14, at once betrays the great passion of Dorothy's life:

"William and John set off into Yorkshire after dinner at half-past two o'clock, cold pork in their pockets. I left them at the turning of the Low-Wood bay under the trees. My heart was so full I could hardly speak to W., when I gave him a farewell kiss. I sate a long time upon a stone at the margin of the lake, and after a flood of tears my heart was easier. The lake looked to me, I know not why, dull and melancholy, and the weltering on the shore seemed a heavy sound.... I resolved to write a journal of the time till W. and J. return, and I set about keeping my resolve, because I will not quarrel with myself, and because I shall give William pleasure by it when he comes again...."

"Because I will not quarrel with myself!" She is full of such illuminations. Here is another:

"Sunday, June 1st.—After tea went to Ambleside round the lakes. A very fine warm evening. Upon the side of Loughrigg *my heart dissolved in what I saw*."

Now here is her account of a country funeral which she reads into, or out of, the countryside:

"Wednesday, 3rd Sept.— ... a funeral at John Dawson's.... I was affected to tears while we stood in the house, the coffin lying before me. There were no near kindred, no children. When we got out of the dark house the sun was shining, and the prospect looked as divinely beautiful as I ever saw it. It seemed more sacred than I had ever seen it, *and yet more allied to human life*. I thought she was going to a quiet spot, and I could not help weeping very much...."

The italics are mine. William was pleased to call her weeping "nervous blubbering."

And then we come to 1802, the great last year of a twin life; the last year of the five in which those two had lived as one soul and one heart. They were at Dove Cottage, on something under £150 a year. Poems were thronging thick about them; they were living intensely. John was alive. Mary Hutchinson was at Sockburn. Coleridge was still Coleridge, not the bemused and futile mystic he was to become. As for Dorothy, she lives a thing enskied, floating from ecstasy to ecstasy. It is the third of March, and William is to go to London. "Before we had quite finished breakfast Calvert's man brought the horses for Wm. We had a deal to do, pens to make, poems to be put in order for writing, to settle for the press, pack up.... Since he left me at half-past eleven (it is now two) I have been putting the drawers in order, laid by his clothes, which he had thrown here and there and everywhere, filed two months' newspapers, and got my dinner, two boiled eggs and two apple tarts.... The robins are singing sweetly. Now for my walk. I *will* be busy. I *will* look well, and be well when he comes back to me. O the Darling! Here is one of his bitter apples, I can hardly find it in my heart to throw it into the fire.... I walked round the two lakes, crossed the stepping-stones at Rydalefoot. Sate down where we always sit. I was full of thought of my darling. Blessings on him." Where else in our literature will you find mood so tender, so intimately, so delicately related?

A week later, and William returned. With him, it seems, her descriptive powers. "Monday morning—a soft rain and mist. We walked to Rydale for letters, The Vale looked very beautiful in excessive simplicity, yet at the same time, uncommon obscurity. The church stood alone, mountains behind. The meadows looked calm and rich, bordering on the still lake. Nothing else to be seen but lake and island." Exquisite landscape. For its like we must go to Japan. Here is another. An interior. It is the 23rd of March, "about ten o'clock, a quiet night. The fire flickers, and the watch ticks. I hear nothing save the breathing of my beloved as he now and then pushes his book forward, and turns over a leaf...." No more, but the peace of it is profound, the art incomparable.

In April, between the 5th and 12th, William went into Yorkshire upon an errand which she knew and dreaded. Her trouble makes the words throb.

> "Monday, 12th.... The ground covered with snow. Walked to T. Wilkinson's and sent for letters. The woman brought me one from William and Mary. It was a sharp windy night. Thomas Wilkinson came with me to Barton and questioned me like a catechiser all the way. Every question was like the snapping of a little thread about my heart. I was so full of thought of my half-read letter and other things. I was glad when he left me. Then I had time to look at the moon while I was thinking of my own thoughts. The moon travelled through the clouds, tinging them yellow as she passed along, with two stars near her, one larger than the other.... At this time William, as I found the next day, was riding by himself between Middleham and Barnard Castle."

I don't know where else to find the vague torment of thought, its way of enhancing colour and form in nature, more intensely observed. Next day: "When I returned *William* was come. *The surprise shot through me.*" This woman was not so much poet as crystal vase. You can see the thought cloud and take shape.

The twin life was resumed for yet a little while. In the same month came her descriptions of the daffodils in Gowbarrow Park, and of the scene by Brothers Water, which prove to anybody in need of proof that she was William's well-spring of poesy. Not that the journal is necessarily involved. No need to suppose that he even read it. But that she could make him see, and be moved by, what she had seen is proved by this: "17th.— ... I saw a robin chasing a scarlet butterfly this morning"; and "Sunday, 18th.— ... William wrote the poem on *The Robin and the Butterfly*." No, beautiful beyond praise as the journals are, it is certain that she was more beautiful than they. And what a discerning, illuminative eye she had! "As I lay down on the grass, I observed the glittering silver line on the ridge of the backs of the sheep, owing to their situation respecting the sun, which made them look beautiful, but with something of strangeness, like animals of another kind, as if belonging to a more splendid world...." What a woman to go a-gipsying through the world with!

Then comes the end…. "Thursday, 8th July.— In the afternoon, after we had talked a little, William fell asleep. I read *The Winter's Tale*; then I went to bed but did not sleep. The swallows stole in and out of their nest, and sat there, *whiles* quite still; *whiles* they sung low for two minutes or more at a time, just like a muffled robin. William was looking at *The Pedlar* when I got up. He arranged it, and after tea I wrote it out—280 lines…. The moon was behind…. We walked first to the top of the hill to see Rydale. It was dark and dull, but our own vale was very solemn—the shape of Helm Crag was quite distinct though black. We walked backwards and forwards on the White Moss path; there was a sky like white brightness on the lake…. O beautiful place! Dear Mary, William. The hour is come…. I must prepare to go. The swallows, I must leave them, the wall, the garden, the roses, all. Dear creatures, they sang last night after I was in bed; seemed to be singing to one another, just before they settled to rest for the night. Well, I must go. Farewell."

Next day she set out with William to meet her secret dread, knowing that life in Rydale could never be the same again. Wordsworth married Mary Hutchinson on the 4th October, 1802. The secret is no secret now, for Dorothy was a crystal vase.

NOCTES AMBROSIANÆ

Weather has sent me indoors, chance to an old book. I have been reading *Noctes Ambrosianæ* again. Bad buffoonery as much of it is and full to the throttle of the warm-watery optimism induced by whisky, yet as fighting literature it is incalculably better than its modern substitute in *Blackwood*. The sniper who monthly tries to pinch out his adversaries there—Mrs. Partington's nephew, in fact—wants the one quality which will make that kind of thing intolerable—that is, high spirits. The Black Hussars of Maga both had them, and drank them, frequently neat. I judge that the Nephew has to be more careful. Eupepsy is not revealed in his writing; but Christopher North and his co-mates must have had the stomachs of ostriches. The guzzling and swilling which were the staple of the *Noctes* were remarked upon at the time as incredible as well as disgusting; but it is to be presumed that they wouldn't have been there if, to the majority at least, they had not been a counsel of perfection. "I wasn't as drunk as I should have liked to be, your Worship, but I was drunk."

As well as that, most people thought it exceedingly funny. Dickens and his readers thought it funny too. Christmas would not have been Christmas unless somebody got beastly drunk. We have moved on since then, and carried the Nephew with us, *multum gementem*. One can see him kicking violently under the arm of the *Zeitgeist* as he is borne down the ringing grooves of change. Now, therefore, he is tart in his musings, chastises rather with fleas than with scorpions.

When the *Noctes* can stand away from Politics and Literature—for the two were always involved in those days, so that unless you approved a man's party you couldn't allow that he wrote tolerable verse—they can wile away a winter evening very pleasantly. Christopher North had an eye for character, a sense of humour, and knew and loved the country. He was country bred. He is at his best when he combines his loves, as he does in the person of the Shepherd. Keep the Shepherd off (*a*) girls, (*b*) nursing mothers, (*c*) the Sabbath, (*d*) eating, (*e*) drinking, (*f*) his own poetry, and he is good reading. Knowing and loving Ettrick Forest as I do, I need no better guide to it than North's Shepherd. Having fished all its waters from Loch Skene downwards, I should ask no better company, evenings, at Tibbie Shields' or the Tushielaw Inn. Edward FitzGerald could have made a good book out of the *Noctes*, cutting it down to one volume out of four. As it is mainly, it will stand or fall by its high spirits. The really funny character in it is Gurney, the shorthand writer, who is kept in a cupboard, and at the end of the last uproarious chapter, when the coast is cleared of the horseplaying protagonists, "comes out like a mouse, and begins to nibble cheese." That is imagination.

The real Ettrick Shepherd was better than the *Noctes* can make him. Lockhart gives a delightful account of his first visit to Walter Scott in Castle Street—his first visit, mind you. He is shown into the drawing-room and finds Mrs. Scott, disposed, *à la* Madame Recamier, on a sofa. His acuteness comes to the aid of his bewilderment, and he is quick to extend himself in similar fashion upon the opposite sofa. In the dining-room he was much more at his ease. Before the end of the meal he had his host as "Wattie" and his hostess as "Charlotte." Next day he wrote to Scott to ask what he might have said, and to offer apologies if needful.

A remark put into his mouth by North, that he could "ban" Burns for having forestalled him with the line—

The summer to Nature, my Willie to me!

set me wondering wherein consists the true lyrical magic. In that line of Burns's, clearly, it lies in the harmony of lyric thought and lyric lilt. In—

Come away, come away, Death,

it is in the lilt alone. One thing only about it is sure, and that is that the diction must be conversational. There will be tears in the voice, but the voice must be that of the homely earth, never of the stage, never of the pulpit If you agree with that, you will have to cut out practically all the poets from Dryden to Cowper, Gray and Collins among them; for Gray has a learned sock, and hardly allows familiarity when he is elegising Horace Walpole's cat. But Shakespeare proves it, Ben Jonson proves it, and all the good poets from Wordsworth. Burns had the vernacular to help him, and for the most part a model to steer by. All Lowland Scots, lads and lassies, wail, and occasionally howl, in his songs. The first two lines of that one envied by Hogg run:

Here awa, there awa, wandering Willie,
Here awa, there awa, haud awa hame!

and of these the second is traditional, altered only in one word. Burns writes "haud awa hame" instead of repeating "here awa"—and improves it. Shakespeare used the King's English, but never shirked a racy idiom. Here is a good instance from the Sonnets, and from one of the greatest of them, "Farewell, thou art too dear."

> Thus have I had thee as a dream doth flatter—
> In sleep a king; but waking *no such matter*.

You might call that a slang phrase and be right.

There are other cases, and many; some where he goes all lengths, and one at least where he goes beyond them. But to leave Shakespeare, for a perfect example of passion married to common speech, commend me to—

> Since there's no help, come let us kiss and part,
> Nay, I have done, you get no more of me;
> But I am glad, yea, glad with all my heart
> That thus so clearly I myself can free.

Intense feeling, intense music, a lovely thing: a poem.

SKELETONS AT A FEAST

The other day the village was celebrating the birthday of its Labourers' Union in a manner which used to be reserved for the coming of age of the Squire's son, or for the Harvest Festival, in which the farmer might give thanks for the harvest, and the peasant, perhaps, for having been allowed to assist in winning it. I take a sort of pride in recording a staidness in the observance which I believe to be peculiar to the countryside in which I live. There was a service, with a sermon, in church, all persuasions uniting; then a dinner with speeches; then sports and dancing on the grass. Every stave of the Pastoral was announced and punctuated by the village band. "God save the King" closed all down at nine o'clock.

It was sober merry-making after our manner, yet one could feel the undercurrent of a triumph not difficult to understand. Not a man there but knew, or had heard his father tell, of how things used to be. Ten years ago those men were earning sixteen shillings a week for twelve hours a day; fifteen years ago they were earning twelve shillings; thirty years ago they were earning nine shillings; a hundred years ago they were on the rates, herded about in conscript gangs under the hectorings of an overseer. Now— and it has seemed to come all in a moment—the humblest of them earn their 36_s._ 6_d._; the head men their 40_s._; their hours are down to fifty for the week, with a half-holiday on Saturday; delegates of their kind sit at a board in Trowbridge face to face and of equal worth with delegates of their employers. All matters affecting their status, housing, terms of employment can be brought before the board; and beside that, and behind it, like a buttress, there is a Union, whose name recalls that other grim fortress to which alone in times bygone they had to look when old age was upon them. This new Union has been in existence here little more than a twelvemonth, but they know now that it has spread all over England.

They know more than that. They know that this plexus of organisations is not only social, but political; they feel that the estate of the realm which they stand for may soon become, and must before long become, the predominant estate. They feel the rising tide already lifting them off their feet. The elders are sobered by the flood; but the young ones taste the salt water sprayed off the crest of the wave and look at each other, laugh and cheer. If they rejoice they have good reason, knowing what they know; and if I rejoice with them, I think that I have good reason too. This time seven years ago I sang at length of Hodge and his plow; and looking back and forth over his blood-stained, sweat-stained and tear-stained history, I seemed to see what was coming to him as the crown of his thousand years of toil.

> I look and see the end of it,
> How fair the well-lov'd land appears;
> I see September's misty heat
> Laid like a swooning on the corn;
> I see the reaping of the wheat,
> I hear afar the hunter's horn,
> I see the cattle at the ford,
> The panting sheep beneath the thorn!
> The burden of the years is scor'd,
> The reckoning made, Hodge walks alone,
> Content, contenting, his own lord,
> Master of what his pain has won.

And so indeed it is. The peasant now has his foot on the degrees of the throne, and has only to step up, he and his mates of the mine, the forge, the foundry and the railroad—to step up and lay hand to the orb and sceptre.

If I had misgivings, and if those, when imparted to, were shared by an old friend of mine who still gives me six hours a day of his strength and skill when the weather and his rheumatics can hit it off together, I may say at once that though they were renewed in me by the late threat of the railwaymen arrogantly hurled at the only Government in my recollection which has made arrogance in asking almost a necessary stage in negotiation, they had been present for a long time—beyond Mr. Smillie's wild proposals of direct action, beyond the Yorkshire miners and the flooded coalfields; back to the day when electricians refused to light the Albert Hall, and Merchant Seamen refused passage to some politician or another because they didn't like his politics. One and each of those direct and unsteady actions made me shiver for the men with their feet on the throne's degrees. And now a Railway Strike, which has injured every one and will throw back the railwaymen and their Labour Party for many a year! If these things are done in the green wood, I asked my friend, what will be done in the dry?

He couldn't answer me but by asking in his turn questions which were but a variation of my own. He said: "Our people don't seem to understand anything but 'each man for himself.' The miners hold up the country for higher wages, and the country has to pay them; the railwaymen do the same, and the country must find double fares and high freight. They hit their own class hardest of all, because dear coal and high tariffs touch everybody. And they don't even help themselves, because directly wages are raised, up goes the price of everything. Now what I want you to tell me is how are they going to stop all that when they are the Government? For it will have to stop."

He is right: it will have to stop; but I don't see how the Labour Party is going to stop it. So far as I can make out, the Labour Party, as a responsible, political body, has no control whatsoever over the trade unions; and the trade unions, as such, none over their members. How, then, is one to look forward with comfort to the establishment of a Labour Government? It will take a readier speech than even Mr. Webb's, a more confident than even Mr. Smillie's to illuminate this smoke-blurred scene whereon we make out every trade union preying upon Mr. George's vitals (which are, unfortunately, for the moment our own vitals), and with a success so disastrously easy as to make any prospects of a return to sane, honest, dignified or just government almost hopeless! Mr. George is destroying himself hand over fist, and the sooner the better; but one does not want to see England go down with him. I am all for anarchy myself when once it is thoroughly grasped by everybody that anarchy means minding your own business. But we are far from that as yet. Anarchy at present means minding, and grudging, other people's business. Such anarchy is not government, but plundering with both hands.

My point, however, is that, if we are to have a Labour Government, it must be a Government of a nation, and not a class-affair. When the Duke said that the King's Government must be carried on, he meant the Government of King George or King William. Our present Prime Minister means the Government of Mr. George, which is a very different affair. In its way of simple egotism it is precisely the meaning of the trade unions, and can be shortlier put as "After me the deluge." And that won't do. We want neither autocracy nor anarchy; and just now the one involves the other.

A COMMENTARY UPON BUTLER

Mr. Festing Jones has written a large book about his friend, and written it very well.[A] It is candid, and it is sincere; the work of a lover at once of Butler and of truth; it neither extenuates the faults nor magnifies the virtues of its subject so far as the author could perceive them; and it makes it possible to understand why Butler was so underrated in his lifetime, though not at once why he was so overrated after his death. That remains a problem which cannot be resolved by saying that his friends trumpeted him into it, or that posthumous readers enjoyed seeing him belabour his betters, which his contemporaries had not. It is true that *The Way of All Flesh* did not appear until he was dead, and also true that *The Way of All Flesh* is a witty and malicious novel, whose malice and wit Mr. Shaw had prepared London to admire. Perhaps it is true, once more, that we are more scornful of the old orthodoxy than our fathers were, and less careful whose feelings are hurt. But I must confess that I should not have expected any age to be so complacent about caricaturing one's father and mother as our own was. However, for those who admire that sort of thing—and there must be many—I doubt if they will find it better done anywhere, with more gusto or more point. Dickens is believed to have put his father into *David Copperfield*, not, I think, his mother. But one can love Mr. Micawber, and Dickens would not have so drawn him without love. We are led to Butler's favourite distinction between *gnosis* and *agapé*. There's no doubt about the *gnosis* that went to the making of Theobald and Christina. But where was *agapé*?

[Footnote A: *Samuel Butler, Author of "Erewhon"* (1835-1902): *a Memoir*. By Henry Festing Jones. Two Vols. Macmillan, 1919.]

Butler was in many respects a fortunate man, and should have been a happy one. He had a good education, good health, a sufficiency of means. Even when his embarrassments were at their heaviest he could always afford to do as he pleased. He could draw a little, play a little, write more than a little; he loved travel, and covered all Southern Europe in his time; he had good friends, a good mistress, a faithful servant; he had a strong sense of humour, feared nobody, had a hundred interests. Why, then, did he think himself a failure? Why was the sense of it to cloud much of his writing, and much of Mr. Jones's biography?

He had his drawbacks—who has not? He did not get on with his father, criticised his mother; his sisters scraped the edges of his nerves; a man to whom he was extremely generous betrayed him. The like of these things must happen to mortal men. Butler knew that as well as any one. But his books were not read; the great men whom he attacked ignored him. He thought himself to be something, they treated him as nothing, and the public followed them. He knew all about it, and Mr. Jones knows all about it. He had unseated the secure with *Erewhon*, outraged the orthodox with *Fairhaven*, flouted the biologists, himself being no biologist, plunged into Homeric criticism without archæology, swum against the current in Shakespearianism, enjoyed himself immensely, playing *l'enfant terrible*, and treading on every corn he could find—and then he was angry because the sufferers pretended that they had no corns. How could he expect it both ways? If he was serious, why did he write as if he was not? And if he had tender feelings himself—as he obviously had—why should he expect all the people he attacked with his pinpricks to have none? It was not reasonable.

The answer to these questions is to be found in some little weaknesses of his which Mr. Jones's biography, all unconsciously, reveals. Butler, it is clear, was morbidly vain. Many writers are so, but few let their vanity take them so far. Learn from Mr. Jones. In 1879 he and Butler met Edward Lear in an inn at Varese. He told them a little tale about a tipsy man from Manchester—rather a good little tale. "I do not remember that Edward Lear told us anything else particularly amusing, but then neither did we tell him anything particularly amusing. Butler was seldom at his best with a celebrated man. He was not successful himself, and had a sub-aggressive feeling that a celebrated man probably did not deserve his celebrity; if he did deserve it, let him prove it." There is no getting away from that symptom, which is as unreasonable as it is perverse. Celebrated men are not usually so anxious to "prove" their celebrity as all that comes to. It is bad enough to be "celebrated." It was hard lines on old Lear to sulk with him because he would not show off. If he had wanted to do that he would not have gone to Varese. But that is mortified vanity. The same thing happened when he met Mr. Birrell at dinner in 1900. Then it was the celebrity who took pains to save his host and hostess from a frosty dinner party. The same thing is recalled of meetings with Sir George Trevelyan and Lord Morley earlier in the book. It is all pretty stupid; but when a man is ridden by a vanity like that there can be no healthy pleasure to be got out of writing for its own sake. You must have your public flat on its back before your vanity will be soothed.

Another failing of Butler's, shared, I am sorry to say, by Mr. Jones, was a love of little jokes and an inability to see when and where they could be worked off, or perhaps I ought to say when they were worked out. A great many of them were pinpricks rather than jokes; he only made them "to annoy." Well, they did, and they do, annoy—not because they were jokes, but because they were feeble jokes. "If it is thought desirable to have an article on the *Odyssey*, I have abundant, most aggravating and impudent matter about Penelope and King Menelaus"—so he wrote to Mr. H. Quilter, who naturally jumped at it. Here is another gem which Mr. Jones seems to admire: "There will be no comfortable and safe development of our social arrangements—I mean we shall not get infanticide, and the permission of suicide, nor cheap and easy divorce—till Jesus Christ's ghost has been laid."

All that can be said for that is that it is vivacious, and that it has helped Mr. Shaw, who has certainly bettered the instruction. There are others which are a good deal more annoying than that. Jokes about infanticide and Jesus Christ defeat themselves, and always will. They are on a level with jokes about death or one's mother; they recoil and smite the smiter on the nose. I confess that I find the joke about Charles Lamb irritating. Butler said that he could not read Lamb because Canon Ainger went to tea with his (Butler's) sisters. His gibes at Dante are as bad—in fact they are worse, aggravated by the fact that, having never read (he assures us) a word of him, he puts him down as one of the seven humbugs of Christendom. He would not read Dante because he had liked Virgil, nor Virgil because Tennyson liked him. "We are not amused," as Queen Victoria said of another little joke.

The correspondence with Miss Savage, again, does not reveal a pleasant personality. Indeed, the discomfort one gets from it is at times painful. Mr. Jones says that she bored Butler, and I don't wonder at it. The wonder would rather be that she did not set his teeth on edge if it were not that he was nearly as bad as she was. It is not a matter of facetiousness—I dare say he never tired of that; and perhaps the thinness of the jokes—little misreadings of hymns, things about the Mammon of Righteousness, and so on—in a kind of way added to the fun of them. It is their subject matter which offends. They commonly turn upon the health of the respective parents and the chances of an attack carrying them off. *Queste cose*, as the hero said of the suicide, *non si fanno*. But I suppose that if you could put your mother's death-bed into a novel, you could do almost anything in that kind.

I am myself singularly moved, with Coventry Patmore, to love the lovely who are not beloved—but not the unlovely. Those little jokes, and many others, are by no means lovely, and if Butler repeated them as often as Mr. Jones does, it is not surprising that he was avoided by many who missed or dreaded the point. His lecture on the *Humour of Homer* made Mr. Garnett unhappy and Miss Jane Harrison cross, Mr. Jones says. I don't doubt it. It is very cheap humour indeed, and no more Homer's than mine is. It is entirely Butler's humour about Homer, a very different thing. Its impudence did not mitigate the aggravation, but made it more acute. If he had picked out a fairy-tale, rather than two glorious poems—*Little Red Riding Hood*, *The Three Bears*, *Rumpelstiltskin*, for example—he could have been as facetious as he pleased. But that would not suit him. There would have been no darts to fling. Butler was a *banderillero*. All right; but then don't complain that the Miss Harrisons, Darwins, and others shake off your darts and go about their business, which, oddly enough, is not to gore and trample the *banderillero*; don't be huffed because you are held for a *gamin*. Butler wanted it both ways.

The conclusion is irresistible that Butler's controversial books were not primarily written to discover truth, but because he was vain and wished at once to be sensational and annoying. He resented the greatness of the great, or the celebrity of the celebrated; his vanity was wounded. He sought, then, for "most aggravating and impudent matter" to wound them in turn who had vicariously wounded him. He "learned" them to be toads, or celebrities, or tried to. But his love of little jokes betrayed him. He, a sort of minnow, thought to trouble the pool where the great fish were oaring at ease by flirting the surface with his tail. It seemed to him that he was throwing up a fine volume of water; but the great fish held their way unconscious in the deep. Chiefly, therefore, he failed with all his cleverness. Brain he had, logic he had; the heart was a-wanting and the intention faltered. *Gnosis* again and *agapé*!

Brain he had, logic he had; but brain must follow upon emotional intention if it is to create; and logic must follow upon sound premisses if it is to convince. Now if his prime intention was to annoy, or, if you granted him his premisses, Butler would never miss the mark. But is that intention worthy of more than it earned? I don't think so. And can you grant him his premisses? I don't think that you can. He argued *a priori*, apparently always. I am not a biologist, nor was he, but if I know enough of scientific method to be sure that biologists cannot argue that way, so undoubtedly did he. What should Darwin, who had spent years in patient accumulation of fact, have to say to him? In Homeric criticism—*a priori* again. He had an instinct—he owns it was no more—that the *Odyssey* was written by a woman. Then he studied the *Odyssey* to prove that it was. Perhaps a woman did write it, and perhaps it will one day be proved. The *Odyssey*, as Butler used it, will never prove it. So also with the Sicilian origin of the poem. He got his idea, and went to Trapani to fit it in. It does not seem to have occurred to him that all the things he found there are to be found also in the Ionian Islands and might be found in half a hundred other places in a sea pullulating with islands or a coast-line cut about like a jigsaw puzzle. But it won't do, of course. No one knew that better than he.

Mr. Jones says that "Butler's judgments were arrived at by thinking the matter out for himself." I don't know what judgments he means: in the context he is talking about "other writers." Among such he would not, perhaps, include Dante, Virgil or Charles Lamb. If he includes Homer and Shakespeare there would be a good deal to say. I don't believe he had thought about the authorship of the *Odyssey* at all until he had assumed what he afterwards spent his time and pains in supporting. As to Shakespeare's age when he wrote his Sonnets, I don't myself find that the Sonnets support him. Those which he quotes in particular show that W.H. was a youth, but not that the author was. But there, again, he was arguing *a priori*. He desired to prove what he set out to prove, and the scholars disregarded him. Mr. Bridges, in a letter which Mr. Jones has the candour to quote, puts the matter as neatly as may be. "I am very sorry indeed that you have been so clever as to make up so good (or bad) a story: but I willingly recognise that no one has brought the matter into so clear a light as you have done. You are always perspicuous, and nothing but good can come of such conscientious work as yours. Still, you must remember that you proved Darwin to be an arch-impostor; and there was no fault in your logic. It is not the logic that fails in this book." No. It was not the logic.

THE COMMEMORATION

Eleven o'clock in the morning found the village at its field and household affairs, with birds abroad and dogs at home assisting in various ways. The plovers wove black and white webs over the water-meadows, gulls were like drifting snow behind the plow. In a cottage garden the dog, high on his haunches at the length of his chain, cocked his ears towards the huswife in the wash-house, hoping against hope for a miracle. Luxuriously full, the cat slept on the window-ledge. Meantime a roadman was cleaning a gutter, a thatcher pegged down his yelm; a milkmaid, driving up the street in a float, stopped, threw the reins over the pony's quarters, and jumped down, very trim in her overall and breeches. The church clock struck eleven.

She turned, as if shot, and stood facing the church whose flag streamed to the south. The roadman straightened himself and leaned upon his mattock; the huswife shut the back door, and the dog crept into his barrel. The schoolyard, accustomed at that hour to flood suddenly with noise, remained empty. But the milkmaid's horse drew to the hedge for a bite, the birds on the hillside settled about the halted plow, and the cat slept on.

We are what we are, all of us. Beasts and birds are not sentimental. Things to them stand for things, not for thoughts about things. I have seen young rabbits play cross-touch about the stiffened form of an unfortunate brother. I have seen a barnyard cock flap and crow, standing upon the dead body of one of his wives. Directly a creature is dead it ceases to be a creature at all to those which once hailed it fellow. It becomes part of the landscape in which it lies; and with certain beasts which we are accustomed to call obscene it becomes something to eat. But dogs which have lived long with us are not like that. I knew two dogs which lived in a house together and shared the same loose-box at night. One night one of them in fidgeting, bit upon an artery and bled to death. Never again would the survivor enter that sleeping place. Dogs have learned from us that things may stand for thoughts.

Anything that persuades the British people to spend two minutes a year in thought is a good thing; for thinking is not congenial to us. Feeling is; and feeling may perhaps be described as thinking about thinking. We feel still, as we felt at the time, the wholesale, hapless, heroic and entirely monstrous sacrifice of our young men; but it is out of the question to suppose that we thought about them—or, for that matter, that any nation in the world did; for if we had thought as we felt the scythe would have stopt in mid-swathe and Death been robbed of a crowning victory! But we did not think; and we were not thinking just now when we stood still in the midst of our interrupted affairs. The act sufficed us. It was a sacrament. An act, that is, a thing, stood for a thought about a thing—namely heroic, hapless death. Of such sacraments, maybe, is the kingdom of this world, but not, I am persuaded, the Kingdom of Heaven; and assuredly not of such, nor of any amount of it, will be a League of Nations which is anything more than a name.

The thought, or the feeling, of those two minutes here in the village, or in the city eight miles away, where in full market the same opportunity was taken, was concerned in all human probability, with the hapless dead rather than with means to preserve the living from hapless and unnecessary death; and yet, so curiously are we wrought out of emotion, sensibility and habit, some good besides piety may come out of a memorial Eleventh of November. Pitying, recording, respecting the dead or perhaps the bereaved, it may presently become a fixed idea with us that avoidable death is taboo. It may be borne in upon us on the next occasion when stung pride, outraged feeling or panic fear is sweeping like a plague over our land, that nothing but sorrow and loss was gained by the Four Years War. That is just possible, but no more than that, we being what we are. Yet, unless we learn to think rather of life than of death, there is no other way. As in religion, faith comes before works, and you must fall in love with God if you are to believe in Him, so it is in politics. Emotional conviction must precede action. And the conviction to be established is that war is a crime and in some nations, a vice.

In the Middle Ages a great and ever-present fear of death coincided with an extraordinary neglect of life. Whole companies, whole classes of men thought of little but death; yet they killed each other for a look or a thought; in war whole cities were put to the sword and fire, as the Black Prince put Limoges. *Timor mortis conturbat me!* So men shuddered and wailed, but took not the smallest trouble to keep each other alive. The Black Death swept off at least a third of the population of Europe; yet after it things went on exactly as before. If nations had then possessed the technical skill which they have to-day, it is quite on the cards that France in the Hundred Years or Germany in the Thirty Years War, would have been emptied of its folk. The will thereto was not wanting, that's certain.

Well, we are a little better than that. Sanitation has at last become a fixed idea. And there is another thing. We no longer consider a man as magnified by his office, but rather that the office is magnified in that a man is serving it. In the old days the splendour of an army on the march was reflected upon the men composing it, and glorified every one of them. Now it is the other way. We are apt to see the army glorious because it is composed of men. Lord Kitchener's host, perhaps, has taught us that. We are getting on, then, if we are beginning to take manhood seriously.

It is something at least, and so much to the good, that we have imagined a new sacrament, and found it in the attitude, if not in the act of thought. "Who rises from his prayer a better man, his prayer is answered," said a wise man; and if that is true, the King may save his people yet. But to enable him to do it we must pray for the living rather than the dead, and pray for Good Will among them. For that is what we want.

THE QUAKER EIRENICON

In our late scramble to spend our own, or secure some other body's, money, a message of beauty, distinction and serene confidence in its own truth, has been overlooked by this distracted world. There is little wonder. As well might a blackbird flute on Margate Sands on a Bank Holiday as this Quaker message, "To all men," breathe love and goodwill among them just now. The effect has been much the same: to those who heeded it matter for tears that such heavenly balm should be within our hearing but out of our grasp; to the ravenous and the rabid a mere foolishness.

To my mind nothing so admirable has been put forward by any Church calling itself Christian throughout five years' horror and delirium. I must not expect the *Morning Boast* or *Long Bow* to agree with it, but I am inclined to ask my fellow citizens if they have not yet had enough of these evangelists of war and ill-will towards men. If they have, here is an alternative for them to try.

"We appeal to all men," say the Quakers to the world, "to recognise the great spiritual force of love which is found in all, and which makes us one common brotherhood." It is a hard saying, as things are now; and yet, if it is true, that 'tis love that makes the world go round, it is certain by this time that 'tis hate that makes it stop. What stops trade? English hate Germans, Germans hate English; masters grudge men, men masters. What holds up Ireland? Protestants hate Catholics, Catholics Protestants; each hates England and England hates both. The infernal brew of 1914 has poisoned the tissues of humanity; proud flesh, sour blood, keep us all in a sick ferment. What will save us? Who will show us any good?

One thing only, say the Quakers. Listen. "Through the dark cloud of selfishness and materialism shines the eternal light of Christ in man. It can never perish.... The profound need of our time is to realise the everlasting truth of the common Fatherhood of God—the Spirit of Love—and the oneness of the human race." I wondered on Christmas Day, when children were carolling "Peace on earth and mercy mild," for how many hundred years men had been hearing that, how many of them had said that they believed it, and how many had acted as if they did believe it. I wondered if the editors of *Long Bow* and the *Morning Boast* had heard them, and what effect the words would have upon their next articles about the deportation of aliens, or the value of machine-guns as strike-breakers.

"We have used the words of Christ, but we have not acted upon them. We have called ourselves by His name but we have not lived in His spirit." Those words should form part of any General Confession to be used in church, since the words used there now have lost their meaning. They are entirely true; since Christ died we have never acted upon His words, or attempted for six years at a time "to live in His spirit." How does one do it? The Quakers go on to tell us. "The Divine Seed is in all men. As men realise its presence, and follow the light of Christ in their hearts, they enter upon the right way of life, and receive power to overcome evil by good. Thus will be built the City of God."

While it is plain, then, how the City of God will be rebuilt on earth, it ought to be equally so how it will not be built. Lately another Message has been advertised in the Press, which does not promise any help. It has been proposed[A] to publish certain private letters of the German ex-Emperor which, we learn, incriminate him still more deeply in the original sin of the war. Here no doubt is "a scoop," as they call it, for somebody; but with "scoops," I suppose, the City of God has little to do.

[Footnote A: It was done too.]

And apart from the supposition that the man is about to be tried for his offences against society at large—in which case it is a flouting of justice to publish evidence against him in a newspaper beforehand—apart from all that, how in God's name is His city to be rebuilt by raking in waste-heaps for more hate-stuff? The wretched man is beaten, abdicated, exiled, sick, probably out of his mind, if he ever had one. Is it an English habit to revile the fallen and impotent? It has not been so hitherto, and the newspaper which proposes to enrich itself by making most of us ashamed of our nationality is doing us a bad service and, I hope, itself a worse.

But while such things go on, far from the City of God being rebuilt, the ruins of it will sink deeper into the morass, until we all go down to the devil together. And if we are to be as the Evangelists of Ill-Will desire us, the sooner that happens the better. As an alternative to this disgusting but deserved consummation I call attention to the Quaker Eirenicon.

I love and respect the Quakers as Christians after the doctrine of Christ. I have known many, and never a bad one among them, never one that was not sound at heart and sweet in nature. As well as their social quality there is to be considered their political. I don't hesitate to say that their Corporation holds in its grasp the salvation of the world through their Master and mine. I go further, and don't hesitate to say that had the Quaker religion been this country's, not only should we not have made war, but Germany would not have provoked it. Had Europe at large been Quaker, war would have been eliminated long ago from the catalogue of national crimes; for to a Quaker war is what cannibalism is to all men, and love, apparently to some men, an unthinkable offence against the sanctity of the body. That body, they say, is a possible tabernacle for the Spirit of Christ. If you believe that, all the rest follows. If you do not, you will continue to read the *Morning Boast*.